MARTHA BER

A Farm Under a Lake

"There's a hint of Southern writer Eudora Welty in *A Farm Under a Lake,* and a suggestion of Alice Munro, too. Bergland's writing is close to perfect pitch. The details illuminate [the story] in an almost visionary way, with their attention to how 'mere colors and mere breezes and mere kisses can go through the skin to the heart.'" —*San Francisco Chronicle*

"Like her literary forebear, Willa Cather, who crafted a fictional world of incredible power and beauty from the alien soil of Nebraska, Bergland gently coaxes stories out from the taciturn landscape of [the Midwest of] her youth, a place where neither the land nor the people yield up their secrets or their drama too eagerly." —*Milwaukee Magazine*

"A remarkably dexterous novel...Bergland spins her tale with effortless grace [and] writes with great heart." —*St. Paul Pioneer Press*

"In luminous prose, unmarred by false notes or easy clichés, Bergland tells the tale of a woman as recognizable as a sister or oneself, who finds her life different from what she had expected it to be—and has the courage to examine how and why. Bergland's delicate but unflinching touch extends from character to setting.... This fine first novel is marked in all aspects by deftness, honesty and compassion." —*Publishers Weekly*

A Farm
Under a Lake

A   N O V E L   B Y

M A R T H A   B E R G L A N D

VINTAGE CONTEMPORARIES

VINTAGE BOOKS

A DIVISION OF RANDOM HOUSE, INC.

NEW YORK

FIRST VINTAGE CONTEMPORARIES EDITION, DECEMBER 1990

Copyright © 1989 by Martha Bergland

All rights reserved under International and Pan-American
Copyright Conventions. Published in the United States by Vintage
Books, a division of Random House, Inc., New York, and distrib-
uted in Canada by Random House of Canada Limited, Toronto.
Originally published in hardcover by Graywolf Press in 1989.

Library of Congress Cataloging-in-Publication Data
Bergland, Martha, 1945-
A farm under a lake : a novel / by Martha Bergland.
—1st Vintage contemporaries ed.
p.   cm.—(Vintage contemporaries)
ISBN 0-679-73011-7
I. Title.
PS3552.E71925F3   1990
813'.54—dc20   90-50170
CIP

Intaglio prints by Susan Moran

Manufactured in the United States of America
10 9 8 7 6 5 4 3

Contents

To the memory of my grandmothers –

Ida Martha Hoover Howard

and

Eloise Beal Bond Bergland

A Farm Under a Lake

Foot in the Road

Jack is the church I have joined, but he is a church without ceremony. I miss my old church; I miss the gathering together and the celebration and the incense, the songs and the clearing of air. I think I said this out loud in the driveway with my hand on the car door handle which, like everything else, was still wet with dew. I stood a minute and listened to the robins singing their extravagant morning tune in our otherwise silent suburb. It was Saturday and it was June. I was leaving to take May Nickelson down to her daughter's in Illinois. I was about to, as my mother used to say, put my foot in the road. "All you have to do is put your foot in the road," she would say to show how easy change was. My bag was in the back of the car, and so was a thermos of coffee, but I stood there listening to robins. Just get in; just put your foot in the car. I think I said that out loud too. The robins, I realized, reminded me of holiness. On a flat-land

grain farm with no cover around the house and fields full of
pesticides, there weren't many robins, so the ones I remembered
were in Half Moon in the lilac bushes beside the little Catholic
church. The sound of holiness was robins, and the odor of sanc-
tity was lilies of the valley. Here in the suburbs, the mist rose in
wraiths from the asphalt and roofs and hoods of cars. No one
else was out besides me. In the house behind me was my husband, Jack Hawn. I could see Jack as clearly as if he were sitting
at the kitchen table in the yard and I had eyes in the back of my
head. Jack was sitting at the kitchen table in his three-piece suit
and his arms were straight in front of him on the Formica; his
coffee cup was at his right hand and the newspaper, open to the
want ads, was spread out in front of him. The TV was on and
Tom Brokaw and Jane Pauley were laughing. Jack was not. His
face was heavy and worried. He only reminded me of the man I
married.

When I got in the car, my hand was still wet from the dew on
the handle. I sat there. It took me as long to decide to dry my
hand on my skirt as it did for my hand to dry in the air. I was sitting there trying to maintain my weight, my usual heaviness of
heart, my love. I was trying not to lighten myself or to release
myself from anything. I was only going away for four days. I was
going to drive May Nickelson down to Illinois. I was getting paid
for this. Jack was still out of work, so we needed the money.
There was no reason to feel either guilt or relief.

I got out of the car and wiped the dew off the car windows
with my forearm. I dried my arm off on the hem of my skirt,
then got back in the car.

Then I got out of the car and walked back to the house.

In the kitchen, Jack was where I'd left him and as I'd imagined him. Tom Brokaw was interviewing Rosalyn Carter. I stood
behind Jack with my hands on his shoulders – all those layers of
cloth! – and wondered what kind of church Jimmy was. Did

Rosalyn really believe? Then I pulled a chair up close to Jack and put my arms around him. "I love you, Jack. Are you going to be OK by yourself?"

Jack was watching the national weather, the big weatherman. "There's a line of thunderstorms across northern Illinois. Watch it down there, Janet." Jack turned and looked at me. "Is your old lady scared of storms?"

"Watch it down there, Janet"? I could count on four hands the times in the last year that Jack has said my name.

"She isn't my old lady, Jack. She's my job." Actually it was my idea that I drive her down there; her daughter had planned to come get her. But Jack and I grew up in that part of the world, and, though separately — they are divorced — my parents had been up to see us, I hadn't been home to Half Moon or the farm for many years. I wanted to see that part of the world again, not from the point of view of a sexed-up kid, but from that of a working woman. A married woman. I was a private-duty nurse.

"Why can't her daughter come and get her? Why do you always get that kind of job?"

"I'll be back in four days. I'll call you every day. I'll bring you something."

"Bring me one of those." Jack pointed to a Jaguar on the screen. "And bring me a job while you're at it." Jack's posture hadn't changed with talk or with hugging. He sat at our kitchen table as if he were at a desk. He was watching Tom and Jane laugh at a hat with a pig's face on it that the big weatherman was wearing. What was that man's name? In a few years Jack would look just like him. Somebody from here, from Green Bay, Wisconsin, had sent the weatherman the pig hat.

"I do love you, Jack." I stood behind him with my hands on his shoulders counting the layers of cloth down to his skin, counting the tough layers between my hands and my sweet bridegroom, Jack, counting the weeks or months since I had felt Jack's skin under my hands. I imagined my hands tight around Jack's neck. I knew that later I would see this scene and feel it. Later, I would know what I meant.

I stood there, but Jack said nothing. I went to the car, and left.

Now the dew was gone, and now I was going to be late to pick up May, and now instead of lightness as I drove, I felt a heaviness in my neck and shoulders that made me look like my mother. My hands on the steering wheel had the same expression as my mother's. There was a pulling in my chest that I knew from experience would last about forty miles; Jack's sphere of influence seemed to go out forty miles. After that, the signals were too weak and I couldn't pick him up.

Though I was late, I drove slowly beside the bay and saw people already up feeding the seedy-looking geese in the park. I wondered if I could start picking up someone else when I was out of range of Jack. For a moment I thought of Carl; I saw him drinking alone in that empty farm house. But, I am out of range of Carl, and there is no one else. Not any more. I haven't picked up anybody – literally or figuratively – for twenty years. No, that's not true. I did pick up the cabbage man, so I am only *almost* the perfect wife. I was talking to myself again, and I laughed out loud too. I tried to laugh like Jane Pauley but it didn't work.

I used to be a sender. I used to send like Jack does. I used to send and receive. Now I pick up Jack and old ladies, but my foot is in the road.

May Nickelson, whom I'd been taking care of for almost a year, was, in Jack's words "well off." She lived in a big Lannonstone house right on the bay. Apparently she and her husband, who was some kind of manufacturer, lived here together for thirty-some years and raised two daughters, and then after he died, she lived on here alone for almost fifteen years. She kept herself occupied mainly with crafts, it seems, and then she fell on the ice and broke both wrists and her mental condition began to deteriorate. I have been staying with her in the evenings and at night during the week. Another woman stays on the weekends. I was hired to fix her supper, get her ready for bed, then stay with her until the day shift came. But several times lately, May got away from the day nurse and was found walking down the road in her nightgown. And sometimes during the day May would just walk into the young couple's house next door anytime she wasn't being watched. If they locked the house, she'd appear smiling at their windows, and if they forgot and left it unlocked, they would find May curled up on the couch in the den or asleep under the baby's crib. The last straw was one afternoon when the woman went upstairs to check on her baby, heard a noise in their bedroom, and found May in their bed.

Then the social workers were called, and May's daughter and her lawyer, and arrangements began to be made. The house was sold, and the contents were to be sold today, the day I was to drive her and a few of her things down to her daughter's in Quincy, Illinois. The daughter didn't want any of May's things, and she wanted all of this settled.

When I first knew May, she would sometimes come into focus and make a comment about the here and now: "This meat loaf tastes funny," "You shouldn't wear that color, Janet," or "No one should live to be this old." But now, May just smiled. She rarely spoke, though now and then she would mutter vile things to someone named Judy and someone else named Fritz. Once she flew off the handle and threw a whole rack of coffee mugs one at a time across the kitchen, cracking the glass in the oven door and breaking the window over the sink. I was on the other side of the counter in the dining room, and, I have to say, the scene gave me a thrill that I am still ashamed of. I ducked down behind the counter, more to keep her from seeing me laugh than to protect myself.

May is the most complicated person I have ever taken care of even though she no longer speaks. She is complicated in the relationship between her appearance and her mental condition, for one thing. May looks wonderful. She is dark complected, she has only a few wrinkles, and she has a lot of naturally curly thick white hair. Her posture is only a little stooped, and she has wonderful legs. Today, at forty, I would like to have the legs of this eighty-one-year-old woman. Her clothes are all cheerful and bright colors. She looks, from a distance, relaxed, happy, smart. It's only after you are with her for a while that you realize she never speaks, the cheerful expression of her mouth and her pale blue eyes is also tentative and bewildered, and it never changes.

She is complicated also because she has both a relentless domesticity and a relentless desire to get out of her house.

I was hired to keep her from wandering out of her house at night, but that's exactly what I've let her do. The social worker and the doctor have been worried at how much she sleeps in the day time, but I know it's because of how little she sleeps at night. She walks at night — summer and winter, in any weather.

At first, every night I would get her ready for bed and try to keep her there. I would fix her warm milk or cocoa, give her a sleeping pill, play soft music, give her a warm bath and rub her back. But she did not get sleepy and she did not stay in bed. I would try to hold her shoulders down in bed and I'd even lie down beside her and put my arms around her, but nothing made her want to stay there. She would get up and stand at the back door and cry, or she would just lie awake. This went on for weeks. One night, in pure exasperation, I said, "OK, God damn you, go!" Barefooted, smiling in her cotton nightgown, she slipped out the back door. I sat there at the kitchen counter for a few minutes hoping she'd get arrested or hit by a car, but then I calmed down and ran after her. I tried to convince her to come back in, but she was walking fast and didn't seem to even know I was there. It was clear that nothing short of picking her up bodily would get her back in the house, but I am smaller than she is. So May walked for two and a half hours in a wide, wide circle, cutting through suburban back yards now and then, but mainly she stayed on the sidewalks. I walked beside her, though sometimes I would find that she was not beside me; she had taken off silently across someone's lawn.

The next night I took trench coats for both of us and shoes for her, and I didn't try to walk beside her; I followed her. In a few days, instead of getting her ready for bed at ten o'clock, I was getting her ready for a walk. And I wore walking shoes to work.

That winter, while standing in the back hallway, I would dress May to go outside as you would a child. I dressed her in heavy pants, snow boots, mittens, parka, hat, and, as I tied a scarf around her mouth and nose, she smiled. Sometimes, as I dressed May for the cold, I would play at being somebody's mother. I would try to imagine what it would feel like to never have shifts off from this dependency, and what I always came to feel was relief. I was glad Jack and I had never arrived at the perfect time or place to have our children in. I imagined that having children would feel as confining to me as all these winter clothes did.

When she got out, May would walk purposefully for a few blocks, and then her pace slowed down and she began to look around. She looked in lighted windows. She usually didn't go into yards, but would stop on the sidewalk and stare in at the light. When she did that I stopped beside her and stared too because somehow that seemed less weird than one old woman staring into a house and a nurse lurking in the shadows.

May seemed to have three routes – a suburban one, a nature

one, and a slum one. In the suburbs she walked on sidewalks; in the parks she stayed close to the water; and in the industrial and poor neighborhoods she walked through alleys.

I never told Jack any of this because he would have raised hell at two women wandering around at night. I know there was danger, but no one ever bothered us. It's amazing how few people you see out at that hour – a few joggers, sometimes kids, a drunk or two, and the cops patrolling. The houses seem to have sucked all human life into them, where it is displayed in yellow or blue light.

I suppose I could have found ways to lock May in the house at night, but I was afraid of what might happen on her face or inside of her when she discovered she couldn't get out. It was a cruelty I didn't see the necessity for.

I tried to understand her reasons, tried to see what she saw, but I didn't really figure it out. Many times, in the quiet of the night, drinking cocoa at the kitchen table with just the stove light on, I asked her, "May, why do you go out there? What do you see?" She never did answer, but she sometimes turned her face toward me at the sound of my voice.

I especially wanted to know what one particular house meant to her. It was one of several houses between a railroad yard and a plumbing supply warehouse. The house and the others near it were small, poor, square, covered in that fake red-brick asbestos siding; they must have been built around the turn of the century for railroad workers. This house was May's turn-around point, the end of what I called her "slum walk" – the only walk with a destination. Though the houses on either side of it were inhabited, and some attempt was made to keep them up, this house was almost obscured by tall weeds in the front yard, a fallen porch roof, and the grass that grew tall in the cracks of the front walk that cut the yard in two. May always walked completely around this house, which meant cutting through the neighbors' yards. Luckily, neither of these neighbors had dogs, and luckily, in the summer, though their windows two feet from us were open, the TVs were usually blaring. So May stood on the walk between the houses and stared into this empty house. It was always dark, the windows were always shut tight, and, in the winter, no footsteps led through the snow into or out of the house. Through windows with no curtains, the streetlights shone on bare floors. She never told me, but I asked May many times, "What is this place to you?" I am a person who doesn't accumulate things I can't use, so maybe at the time I was just as glad she didn't tell me.

My constant sorting and throwing out things was the opposite of May's accumulating. For recreation, I used to clean the basement and garage and all our closets and cupboards and then throw things out or take them to the Goodwill. Except for linens – I did have chests and cupboards full of sheets and towels and tablecloths and napkins – I wanted us to have only what we used or needed, partly because we moved around so much, but anything that had ever come into May's house since around 1950, May still had. She had nothing very old, but she had bought and made and decorated a lot of stuff. She decoupaged plaques and wooden boxes; and she embroidered napkins, tablecloths, dish towels, and aprons. She needlepointed chair seats, cute sayings, curtain tie-backs, hassock covers. She had woven baskets and decorated straw wreaths. She had made quilted blender covers, pot holders, and a cover for her food processor. Every surface had a plastic cover or a doily or an embroidered cloth. Everything useful in May's house was disguised to look like something useless or disguised to look as if it came from an earlier era. May wanted nothing to look like what it was or to show any signs of wear or age. The extra toilet-paper rolls looked like colonial ladies; pot holders were shaped like fish; wreaths like picture hats; hooked rugs like cats and dogs; trivets like geese. The toaster had a cover that looked like a covered bridge with a bouquet of flowers and a bow glued to the roof. In order to do anything in her house, you had to first find things, which meant you had to figure out her coding and disguising system. It was hell to keep things clean, everything you did took twice as long as it should have, and there was no place to rest your eye. In the early mornings, when May was finally asleep, I often wandered around the house trying to imagine it with nothing in it, without the Venetian blinds, sheers, and brocade draperies that obscured the view of the bay. There was something so excessive about May's possessions, something aggressive and hostile about the artificiality. At first, though I hated her taste, I admired her vehemence and thoroughness, but after a while I began to take all her stuff personally. And gradually I began to get rid of it.

I didn't throw anything out, but every day I selected two or three monstrosities and packed them away in boxes or shopping bags and put them away in the attic. May either didn't notice or didn't mind, and I began to find her house not so offensive. As a matter of fact, it was a good house, finished with tasteful and expensive materials and good workmanship. Under the little rugs were good oak floors; behind the plaques and decorated candles on the mantel was a stone fireplace, and, most of all, beyond all those curtains was the bay.

I was gradually exposing the beautiful bones of May's house, I told myself, and I told myself that May must really like it better this way: all that detail and clutter must be confusing to someone in her state of mind. I also told this to the social worker who, like me, couldn't imagine getting anything done in a house with that much in it. Each night, after our walks, usually at one or two in the morning, I packed up one box or bag and put it in the attic, but one night I noticed that more than what I was putting away was disappearing. Maybe I had put those things away and had forgotten, but I looked everywhere and they were nowhere in the house. The woman who stayed on the weekends must be taking things. Either she hated May's stuff even more than I did, or she figured she needed it more than May did.

At first I was upset and thought I'd report this to the police or at least to the agency, but I didn't. May's house was looking nice and, besides, I couldn't prove anything. Then I began to hope that particular items would be stolen, and one Friday I even put the covered-bridge toaster cover in a shopping bag by the door, and, sure enough, on Monday it was gone.

The day I was to take her down to Illinois was also the day of the sale of her household goods.

By the time I got to May Nickelson's that morning, it was nine. The "Today Show" was over which meant that Jack was at that moment making a list on a yellow tablet of the phone calls about jobs he was going to make that day. He had the newspaper want ads carefully analyzed and had ranked the few job openings advertised according to Likelihood of Getting Job and Desirability of Job. He had another list of Letters to Write and one of People to See. I could see Jack earnestly cleaning up the kitchen and then moving into the den where he had set up an office. He was organized, sensible, desperate, and courageous. So why was I so glad I wasn't there? And why did my arms and shoulders ache?

At May's, there were estate-sale signs out front and plastic flags lining the driveway. There were so many cars already there that I had to drive around the block to find a place to park. All of May's things were in the yard on tables in the bright sun, out of context, for anyone to look at. Rugs were on the lawn, bedroom furniture was in front of the garage, and dining-room chairs were lined up beside the front walk. As I walked through this display, I began to feel kind of funny. I was remembering the sale of my family's things, the farm, twenty years before. I tried to take slow breaths as I walked past tables in the yard that held the very boxes and shopping bags of monstrosities that I had packed away and put in the attic. May was made to look ridiculous and trivial – laughable – by being sold piecemeal like this, as we were years before.

In the kitchen, women I didn't know were marking prices on dishes and putting linens in zip-lock bags to be displayed and sold. "Where's May?" I asked one of the women. "Who's 'May'?" the woman responded. "This is her house," I said. "Oh, I'm so sorry, dear. Why don't you see Debby Chapman in the dining room." She took my arm. I must have looked a little green or at least intense.

Debby Chapman had a name tag on and was sitting at the dining-room table as if it were her desk. She was writing on a clipboard.

"Where is May Nickelson?"

"The owner? Oh, I'm so glad you came for her. This can be upsetting for them and for our girls, too. They don't usually have to see the owners. She's upstairs. Go on up."

Dark patches on the sun-bleached wallpaper told what had been hanging on the stairway walls and for how long. The patches were darkest at the bottom of the stairs, lightest at the top. May had decorated from the bottom up, so going upstairs was going forward in time to the most recent past. This felt backwards to me and I wondered why.

I resented being given permission to go upstairs in a house I had worked in for a year, a household I'd really managed for a year. It felt like *my* house and I realized that May *was* my old lady. She was my job, but she was my old lady, and I loved my job. Her house was even more mine than old Mr. Maclean's had been; she was even more mine than Mr. Maclean was. I loved to go into her house and the houses of other old people who lived alone; I would smooth things out and help them stay there. I loved to see the people feel safe and comfortable because of me. I would go into the homes of widows who slept fearfully and fitfully for years, and then watch them sleep deeply because they were not alone. I waited on women for whom nothing had been brought or fixed for decades. I put my arms around people who had felt nothing heavier on their arms than cloth for years. I watched them at first guard their gratitude because my gestures had so exposed their loneliness. I saw them come to believe in my help, then expect it. I realized that when old people because of me—and their money, as Jack said—could die peacefully in their homes and not be carted off somewhere, then I had succeeded. What was happening to May today was the kind of thing I had worked against for years.

I don't know. Maybe this sadness was just because May's house felt like my house. It was a haven for me. I came here so often from my own home rattled, dissatisfied, incomplete, angry, a mess. But after I was here with May for a while, I settled down; I was fine. I knew what to do. Here I was competent. Here I could read so well the voiceless body of May, as I could the bodies and voices of all the other old strangers I took care of. How is it that I could understand these strangers and yet not be able to tell if my husband loves me, if the anger in his voice is at me? I was more at home here in May's house than in my own bed. This was my house.

I loved to do for strangers what I wanted to do for Jack.

May was upstairs in her bedroom. She was standing at the window, not looking out at the bay, but facing in. I looked at her for some sign that she knew or felt what was happening to her, but there was none. Her expression was that same half smile.

"May," I said, "I'm going to run your bathwater now. Why don't you get undressed? Pretty soon I'll tell you what's going on." I didn't trust myself to speak more at that moment, I was so sad.

I turned the water on and, while the bathtub filled, I got out her clean underwear and slip and laid out three dresses on the bed. Sometimes she could choose if she didn't have to speak. While May undressed, I finished packing the few things we would take with us in the car.

May stood in the middle of the room and took off her slippers and robe and nightgown the way a four-year-old would, only slower. May was not modest or immodest. She was as comfortable naked as clothed. I have seen many bodies in my work and I have seen that age degrades most bodies, but May was somehow idealized by age. I don't mean that she looked like a movie star – gravity had taken its toll on her – but her body was always sweet-smelling and pretty and clean as though she were through with the striving and sweating that make the rest of us stink and worry. Her skin was smooth, dry, the few wrinkles delicate like silk. When I sat on the edge of the tub to test the water, May always stood next to me and put her hand on my shoulder to steady herself when she got in the tub. She loved the bath. I'm not sure how I know this because she never said so, but I guess you can tell what a cat loves, too, without a cat telling you so. May loved it when I washed her and she loved the feel of the water. Sometimes she masturbated in the bath. At first I had pushed her hand away from herself, but later on I would just turn around and look out the window at the trees in the hedge.

After her bath, when she had put on her underwear, slip, and stockings, I asked May if she wanted to choose which dress to wear. Today she understood me and walked over to the bed where I'd laid out a blue one, a pale green one, and one with pink flowers. May stood in front of each dress momentarily as if it were a doorway she might go through. She put her hand on the cloth of each dress. She picked up the flowered one, soft pink flowers on much-washed cotton, and she held it to her body with both arms. Her expression changed a little. I hadn't seen this happen in months. I stood barely breathing on the other side of the bed watching for more tiny changes of expression. Then, after a moment, her smile became more inward. She was seeing something. Her hands on the cloth were reading something, remembering. I watched her face; I was as hungry for expression as a farmer is for rain. I didn't want to scare this away, but I leaned towards her.

"May," I said quietly, "what is it? What do you see?" I waited. She was remembering something. Something was moving over her face as sun and cloud shadows move on a field.

"May, please, what do you see? Tell me." Her smile went deeper. There were tears in her eyes. I was seeing something almost extinct.

"Please, May, talk to me. Tell me. The dress. Where were you? Where are you?"

May was holding the dress in front of her face. She put her face in the cloth. "Oh," she said. "Oh." She closed her eyes and almost fell onto the edge of the bed. She sat holding the dress, remembering. Though my knees were shaking, I went around the bed to where she sat, and I knelt in front of her, my hands holding her hands which held the dress.

"May, please talk to me. Tell me what you see. Please, May." I was looking up at her face. She was looking out the window at the bay.

"Mrs." May whispered.

She still looked across the water. "Mrs. who?" I finally asked.

There was no answer. "Tell me, May. Tell me something. I'll tell you everything. Mrs. who?"

I watched her. She turned her face toward me and looked at me. It took my breath away: Not only was she truly smiling, but she looked amused and she was looking at me, into my eyes. The real May then said to me, "Mississippi. The Mississippi River."

She was looking at me, Janet Hawn, her nurse, in my face, in my eyes. I looked and looked at May, but her looking back imperceptibly faded as light leaves a field and then she was just smiling, gone.

I waited a few minutes. I watched her face for signs that she would remember again and be here, but there were none. "Come back, damn it, May. Let me in. Don't leave me out here. You can't do this." There was no answer.

I cried for a while on that pink dress she held in her lap. May was beautiful, full of stories, secrets, memories, reasons, but she was inaccessible to me. She was the center of my life, with Jack, and both of them were locked up tight. Somewhere locked away was the Jack I married, the gentle and attentive man who smelled like fields, not aftershave and spray starch and antiperspirant. Locked away was the Jack who saw me and desired me. And locked away was the girl who married Jack, who wanted him, who loved him on all her skin. I wanted back in. I wanted us both back. I wanted to go home.

After a while I wiped my eyes on May's pink dress and I held her hands tight, maybe I hurt her, and I said: "Listen, May, you are leaving your home today. You will never come back here. You will never again see this house, this view of the water, your kitchen, all the things you made. Never. This is the house where you lived with your husband and raised your girls. Now it belongs to a stranger. It's been sold. And right now your things that you made are being sold to more strangers and will be scattered all over and some of the things that you made with your own hands will be sold in those junk stores on Washington Street. I am taking you down to Illinois to live in one room at your daughter's. She is a good woman, but, May, you are leaving your home. May, know some of this; feel some of this." But May didn't. She just smiled.

In a few moments, May and I walked through her house and through the things in the yard as though we were walking through a stranger's yard sale. We got in the car and drove south. May never looked back.

It was only stuff, my mother would say. She's right, it's only stuff. It wasn't her life May was leaving then, or her husband. It was only stuff. May sat beside me in the car, apparently calm and content. She was going somewhere. Her foot was in the road.

I don't know. While May had taken her bath earlier, I had stood at her bathroom window with my arms on the sill and rested my forehead on the screen. Summer was so clear to me, so accessible. The cool, dry breeze had dried off the dew, and the cedar hedge between her house and the neighbor's was full of breezes and sparrows and the lapping sounds of the bay and the raucous first locust of the year. The sky was the blue that makes you smell lakes, and clouds were sailing on like kingdoms. Every surface of the cedars and the wild cherry and grass and the lilacs and globe thistles was susceptible to the breeze. I could breathe in summer. And the goldfinches' songs were like gold bracelets in the trees. I could wear summer on my skin. Maybe this is enough for us. It is a lot.

CHAPTER 2

The Drive

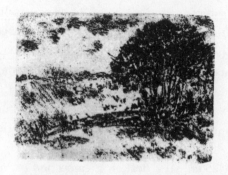

I drove south on the interstate most of the day with May silent
beside me. We listened to the radio some, but May seemed interested, as I was, in the green rolling hills of Wisconsin, the
stone houses, round barns, and the sweet clover and purple
vetch and daisies blooming in the fields and by the roads. We
just drove and I don't think either one of us thought about anything for a long time except here we are driving down the road
on a nice day.

I did begin to talk to May though. At first my talk to her was
just functional: "Is that too much air?" or "Would you rather I
turned the radio off?" I, of course, had to answer my own questions to May because she would not speak and gave me few
signs; I had been doing that all along with May, but there in the
car it began to be different; I began to understand her in a way I
hadn't before. I began to believe my interior answers to my own

questions in a way I hadn't before. I began to hear her voice; I was imagining what she might say — not just the message she might send, the content, but the words she might say and the sound of them as she spoke. "No, dear, I like the air," and "It's just fools talking to fools on those talk shows." I had always to some extent "put myself in the shoes" of the people I had taken care of as anyone must; you imagine what they must be feeling and you see things from their points of view; you imagine their sensations. But this was different. I wasn't imagining sensations, I was bypassing them; I was hearing May's voice.

The further we traveled, the more clear her voice became to me and my own voice cleared too of all the silt that keeps me from saying what I mean. I talked to May, and instead of just asking her questions, I began telling her things that I remembered as we drove.

I told May about Mrs. Bostwick, someone I hadn't thought of for maybe thirty years. When I was a girl, my third-grade teacher was a widow, a tall, thin, severe woman of about sixty named Mrs. Bostwick. She didn't live in Half Moon where I went to school, but in another little town about ten miles away, so she had to drive, alone, twenty miles a day to and from school. In rural Illinois in the fifties, I don't think there was any crime. Now and then one of the Davenport boys would fondle an unwilling girl at a soft-ball game and get sent away for a month or so, and now and then kids would knock over an outhouse but never a gas station. Though my memory is certainly that of a naive and sheltered girl, I am sure women there were not raped by strangers. Yet Mrs. Bostwick was so frightened that she became a joke. When she drove back and forth on those country roads to school, she drove with a scarecrow beside her — men's clothes she had stuffed with paper and cloth and then tied and pinned in the passenger's seat. She put a man's hat on the scarecrow's head, and not only that, she wore a man's hat.

Clearly, she hoped rapists would think here are two men driving a Buick down a road, but what it looked like even to strangers was a crazy lady with a dummy beside her in the car.

As I was almost finished telling May this story, I realized why I had thought of it and then I was torn between wanting May to be conscious enough to be offended and wanting her to not be able to make the rude connection that I had made.

May was not a dummy though she didn't speak. And I was no Mrs. Bostwick. I wasn't afraid.

I was afraid. But I was the opposite of Mrs. Bostwick. I was not afraid outside my house; I was afraid at home. Jack didn't understand this and I didn't really, but I tried to explain it to May.

I wasn't afraid of Jack. I mean I wasn't physically afraid of Jack. He was a gentle man who would never, never hurt me. It wasn't that. And I don't think I was afraid of being married. That made all kinds of sense to me. I was afraid, I think, of the by-products of our marriage. I was afraid of the kind of combustion that seemed to happen lately when Jack and I were in a room together. I kept thinking of an experiment we did in high-school chemistry: two apparently cold substances – water and phosphorus? – when put together caused a strange frantic motion and terrible heat. Jack and I had chemically changed so that now we were dangerous together. We used to be so calm when we were alone; there was never any great heat or great friction between us; we used to be comfortable.

Now I was afraid of what would happen to us if Jack didn't get a job soon. I was afraid of what would happen to Jack if I said all the things I was keeping to myself. I was afraid of what would happen to me if I never said them. But most of all, I was afraid of Jack's anger and ashamed of myself for my fear. I know most of Jack's anger wasn't directed at me, but I felt it that way. I was a coward whose responses were inappropriate and exaggerated, but I didn't know what to do about it. My responses when he raised his voice were as automatic and chemical as his responses when another idiot didn't hire him.

I tried to explain this to May as I had to Jack, but the reality was both more and less than my words.

I told May about how Jack pulled me towards him when I was away from him and pushed me away when I was near. I told May I didn't know what this push and pull were made out of – depression or love or duty or all of them or something else I'd never thought of. I do know that this was nothing Jack did on purpose or was conscious of, and maybe it was nothing that Jack did at all, but something I did to myself. I wasn't sure. I told May that I'd made friends with Karen and Pat, two women in our neighborhood, but because of Jack's wordless push and pull, I had let them fall out of my life.

I remember one time, a beautiful summer day, I had sat in the grass beside Pat's herb garden while Pat and Karen were digging in the herbs. Pat's garden was a big square with nine squares inside it, and each of these smaller ones was planted with a different herb. I was sitting in the grass watching the two of them – tall, elegant women, generous and funny, women I knew I could love deeply – divide the plants and put some in pots for Karen's new herb garden. They were talking quietly, placing their feet carefully among the plants, stooping here and there to dig up herbs. They looked so nice there, but they seemed far away. The sun was hot. The air smelled of dill and mint. A glass of tea was cool in my hand. The women's voices were gentle. Here was everything that I wished for when I was unhappy in the house with Jack. But crows and swallows crossed and recrossed the square of sky above the yard and when I heard a crow in someone else's yard, I felt like a fish hooked in the bones of the chest to a line that Jack was pulling. I could

have been happy for a while there in that garden with Karen and
Pat, but I had to go home and see Jack.

When I got home, Jack was changing a broken handle on the
patio door – a tedious job – and, as I stood in the doorway both
inside and out, holding little pieces of the handle while he
furiously screwed them on, my eye was drawn out of the yard,
and I wished I was back in Pat's herb garden.

It was easy sitting beside May in the car and breakfast was
fine. We went to a fast-food place, I ordered the same thing for
both of us. She ate a fair amount, went with me to the rest
room, and then we left. We must have looked like fairly normal
people – a woman and her daughter or granddaughter.

But later when we stopped to pee, she wouldn't go into the
gas station rest room. She smiled, but she would not walk into
that rest room with me. I worried the whole time I was in there.
Would she be there when I got out? Would someone kidnap her?
Would she get in someone else's car? But when I came out, she
was right where I had told her to stand. She looked strange
though; she looked as if she thought herself invisible, as if she
would only spring into being when some person or some use
came to her. She reminded me of a liveried chauffeur I had seen
once waiting in the doorway of a boutique for his boss to come
out. He was a small man, splendid in his blue uniform with gold
braid, but he was completely unaware that people might look at
him; he looked no one in the eye; he was isolated by his uncon-
sciousness of all human beings but one. May seemed fragile outside that gas station, surrounded by sun and cement and traffic.

In the supermarket, though, I didn't like May. Because it was
such a nice day, we stopped at lunch time to buy things to make
sandwiches to take to a park. Only in the supermarket did I realize how strange May was. I had never gone anywhere with her
but on walks at night and occasionally to a restaurant where her

smile, her preoccupation, her silence did not seem so out of place. In the supermarket, May seemed crazy. She walked in the aisles as though she were on a lawn. She didn't look at the shelves. She clearly had no reason to be there; she didn't know where she was. She smiled, but she smiled at no one. I felt sorry for her, but I didn't like her.

I had felt that way, too, when I would occasionally take her outside to her own beautiful back lawn to watch the sun set. This lawn sloped like a dream lawn between two rows of knobby, crumbling willow trees down to the bay; each evening the gaudy sunset was framed by those melodramatic old trees. I would sit at the top of this yard, on an elegant patio, and watch the sun set beyond the wide expanse of bright green grass, beyond the black and silver bay, and beyond the black trees on the far shore. But May would not sit down and she would not look at the sky. She paced around on the lawn below, looking at the ground or her feet. I tried many times to aim her at the sky or the bay, but, like a cat, she would not be aimed. She was looking at where her feet would be. Her hands were clasped in front of her bodice or she pulled her sweater shut tight and smiled that smile. From where I sat and in the face of the sunset, she was small and silly. Though a great ore carrier slid along as black and as high as the far shore, and though the sailboats ventured almost up to her lawn, May still stood facing her house or the ground, black against the path of the sun on the water. Against the dark shore, under that fuchsia and pale green and mustard sky, the white sailboats were unthinkable thoughts for May.

I couldn't leave May in the car. I didn't trust her. I wasn't sure enough of what she would do or not do. In order to take care of her, I had to keep her with me, so we didn't go to any more supermarkets or gas station bathrooms. I bought toilet paper and we peed in the bushes. I had to show May how to do this, and, when I demonstrated, she laughed out loud at the sight, which I would have enjoyed more had it not been me she was laughing at.

It was a Saturday afternoon in June, so in almost every one of the towns we drove through, we saw a wedding party leaving a church or a procession of cars gracelessly honking and hogging the road. I told May about the funny Catholic wedding processions in Half Moon, but first I told her about Half Moon, which was a pretty little town, a town built on five hills that rose up out of the flat land beside a curve, almost a reverse, in the Sugar River. Half Moon's hilly brick streets and sidewalks were, and probably still are, heaved up and down by frost and the roots of big trees, but we Catholics — a minority in that Protestant town — used to march our weddings the eight or nine blocks up from St. Rose's to the Half Moon — a big, old white hotel with a porch across the front.

The bride and groom always led the procession, the bride carrying her train and veil like ironing over her arm. The groom usually wore pale green or lavender. Little flower girls followed them, swirling their hips, whirling their stiff long skirts around them like hula hoops. A ring bearer, a miniature of the groom, followed at a good clip whacking a satin pillow on his thigh. Matched and mismatched pairs of bridesmaids and groomsmen followed, watching their footing on the sidewalk. The recently lifted weight of ceremony lightened their faces, their feet. Laughing middle-aged mothers took the arms of teen-aged boys they just this day became related to. Fathers were seeing themselves as protectors to an enlarged crop of young women.

The incline, the uneven footing, made this procession raggedy, comic. It was an old joke the town never grew tired of. The absurdity of a bride in expensive white high heels and half-grown boys in rented clothes walking anywhere was part of the joke in a town where no one but the very young and the very old went afoot. In the winter, on icy bricks, this procession was even a better joke. The bride's tulle and lace ballooned above and below her winter coat, and flower girls in pastel hoop skirts and hooded parkas looked like moths half-emerged in the wrong season. Another part of the joke was that, stepping over the heaving tree roots and tripping on the up-ended bricks, the wedding party walked sober like they would later on when they'd had a few. Weddings and funerals were the only time the people of St. Rose's parish played wild Irish Catholic to the rest of the town's temperance Methodist.

In October twenty years ago, Jack and I had been married in Half Moon at St. Rose's and we had marched on those bricks under those trees.

May and I drove a long time that first day. I love to drive and I don't get tired. Sometimes May slept, but mostly she looked out the window, sometimes even turning her head to follow a house or a store or a barn with her eyes. When she was awake, I told her stories. I told her about Jack and I told her about how outrageous I had sometimes been as a girl.

I told her about one Sunday afternoon in the dorm at St. Elizabeth's. JoAnn, my roommate, had just finished giving me a big sermon about how irresponsible and self-centered and conceited I was to treat our friend Margaret like that and steal her boyfriend, Dan. We all thought Dan looked like Marlon Brando and while JoAnn was telling me off I was looking at the Marlon Brando poster behind her on the wall. Marlon, in his black motorcycle jacket and hat, leaned on the handlebars of his bike. He was neither interested nor uninterested, kind nor cruel. He certainly wasn't worried, and I saw then how worried Dan was, and, at that moment, I lost interest in him. I was sitting on the floor in my robe and pettipants and push-up bra. I got up and flounced toward the door. I didn't want to hear any more of this preaching from JoAnn and I didn't want to listen to any more of

Margaret's sniffling. She was lying on my bed crying about Dan. As I got to the door, JoAnn said, "At least I hope you've never slept with him." I turned to her and I said, "JoAnn, for Christ's sake, this is 1965 and I'm almost twenty years old which I'll never be again, and besides that, look at this." Then I flung open my robe and showed them what was then a very pretty body. Both girls gasped. "Do you think I'm going to let this go to waste or wrap it up in tissue paper like farm ladies do their nicest slips and save it for *some* day? *Some day* might never come, JoAnn." Twenty-some years later I was still a little proud of this exit line, and I was proud of what I had looked like, though I wondered what Margaret and JoAnn thought of me and I still hoped they hadn't told anyone that I was sleeping with Dan.

When I remembered my self of twenty years ago, I realized that I saw myself from the back and with a mixture of affection and disgust. I looked smaller, my edges harder, though my face seemed unformed, not yet my own face. I saw myself as though from ten feet behind and I thought of all those awful holy cards of guardian angels hovering behind the two little lost children on the rickety bridge over the ravine. Maybe this is what the nuns meant by guardian angels: the forty-year-old me watching over the twenty-year-old one with nothing to do but smile, or, like those angels, put out a ghostly hand.

I knew, though I didn't tell May, that I was doing this— taking care of old ladies – partly to earn it for myself when I was old. I was forty and trying to take care of the old lady I would be forty years from now. I had no children and neither did my sister, so I always assumed that because my sister was older than I and we're not close anyway, when I am old I will be alone. I have a half-sister, too, though she is more than twenty years younger than I am and I have only seen her twice in my life. She seems less like a sister to me than a daughter I willingly gave up, though someday I may think of her; I may want to know her.

I told May that I never wanted children, that even when I was a girl, I never dreamed of having babies. But I dreamed of being the mistress of a big house with well-stocked pantries and linen closets. I would carry heavy keys and find in my cupboards everything the people in the house needed. Who these people would be, I never bothered to imagine.

I told May about how jealous Jack was — not of a man, because there wasn't any man any more, but of her. Even though she was my job and our only income besides unemployment, Jack was jealous of the amount of time I spent with her and, when I wasn't with her, the amount of time I spent thinking about how to take care of her. Jack was a generous, expansive person when things were going well, but when things were bad, as they have been for the past four years, Jack closed himself down to everyone. He became "self-reliant," he thought; he got rid of excess people in his life, people he couldn't use; he became a cult I had to give up everything for, a fundamentalist church I joined.

I could never picture myself both old and still taking care of Jack. I would rely when I was old, like Blanche DuBois, on the kindness of strangers. I am forty years old; I am taking care of an eighty-year-old woman. I find myself thinking now and then of the newborn girl who will someday take care of me. I tell this girl things in my head and maybe I tell her things out loud. I tell her to remember to speak gently to me and remember to say my name.

We were driving now on two-lane roads through farmland that was like the land around home. The smells of the cornfields and beanfields were the same and so was the feel of the air on my skin. I thought of the farm as it was when I left it and I thought of Orin Check, my grandfather, who died when I was a girl.

If I went back now, there would be almost no sign on the land of the ones who were there and are dead or who have left it, no sign of the past, the rind. The signs that there is a history to the land are small and broken and plowed under: arrowheads, ax-heads, pottery jugs, a white china doll as big as your thumb. The edges of plates, cup handles. Pieces of harness — rusted metal rings and brittle leather. Horse bones. A few brown whiskey bottles. Not much. Roots have been put down deeper in solid rock than they are in this black soil, in this richness. All this agriculture leaves the dead speechless.

What Orin's memory called forth were pictures of the time when the land was fat and ripe and peopled, when men and horses walked on it, when home places were still being built. Orin lived to see the beginning of the tearing down when farms came to support only two crops and fewer and fewer families. He saw the tenant houses torn down, bulldozed out so there wasn't even a clump of weeds around an old pump to show that this is where people lived their lives. Most chalked it up to progress and profit and felt no loss at all. A few, mainly women, saw what Orin Check saw; a few saw what we paid to farm another half acre here and there.

Orin used to want us children to *think* about our well water — brown, rusty, fizzy stuff that we liked to say we hated. He told us our wells went down 175 feet into the Mahomet — an underground river miles and miles wide and older even than the Mississippi. He would say, "You are children who live on a marsh that was drained and over a river that was filled in by glaciers. Stop and think now and then about all that cold water way below you seeping south on top of the bedrock."

Aiming us with his palsied hands on our shoulders, and speaking in a voice full of bitterness and contempt, Orin would point to a piece of field and tell us embarrassed little kids what hired families had lived there, where the house was and the windmill. Over and over he pointed with his wavering arms and voice to what had been pulled down for profit and it was little consolation to him, he said, that the profit was small, if any. Orin Check's voice became more and more unlike the voices of his neighbors. He had set himself up, I guess, as some kind of keeper of lists of the past; his fierce sing-song made us think of him as existing in some other time or religion: "What people make the future up out of is what they play in when they are children. And what they play in when they are children is the past piled up in the lots. Under the saved fence posts leaned up around apple trees, in empty chicken houses, in hedgerows, in willows clogging the ditches, in hog houses. Let it lay. If you tear all that out, what you tear out are places to see from and ways to be."

The three or four years before Grandpa Orin died, his palsy was so bad, he ate his meals in the milkhouse. Grandma carried a tray out the back door, down the steps and across the well platform in any weather three times a day. Orin would not come there until she set down the big bowls of soft food, the jar of coffee, the dish towel for a napkin, and the straws and big spoons. He waited in the barn until she left the milkhouse and until he could see through the kitchen window that she and the rest of us were sitting at the table and eating. Then he left the barn and, in the sidewise way he walked, crossed the lot and went in the back milkhouse door which was always left ajar.

In the house, we ate in silence and tried to ignore the rattling and cursing in the milkhouse. The dogs asleep in the dust woke up and trotted away from the noise, but the cats on the sills and steps always slept through it.

At first it was just the meals out of the house, but at the time he died in his sleep in blankets and hay on the barn floor, he had not been in the house for months. Except for his rages at meal times, he had taken himself from his family and neighbors very quietly. When Grandpa Orin died, we were surprised to realize we hadn't spoken to him for years.

It was evening, I had been driving for hours, and now I was getting tired. May and I had stopped at a supper club and had a good fish dinner in a room overlooking the Rock River. The river was wide and white in the dusk. Now and then logs and snags floated by. The water looked thick. In an earlier life, I used to drive this way from college to home. I still liked these midwestern rivers with substance to them better than the busy, silver rivers of the north. May ate in silence, smiling.

It was almost dark when we left the restaurant for the motel I knew was just down the road. The road ran right along the river. I was driving slowly so I could see the swallows swooping over the water and the shining surface of the water below in its steep banks. The car lights were on. On one side of the road were cornfields; on the other a grove of trees with the white river beyond it.

Ahead of us in the road in the other lane was something. A person? A dog? No, a deer, a small deer. A fawn looking into the grove beside the river. I slowed the car; the deer didn't move. I stopped not far from it, but the deer stayed where it was, looking into the grove. Its legs were oddly splayed, seemed not very efficient, unstable. I flicked my brights off and on to scare it off the road, but it still didn't move. I pulled the car right up next to the deer and rolled the window down. "Get out of the road! Go on home." It didn't move; I should get it out of the road. "Go home!" I said again, but what I really wanted was to see up close this creature – so wild and rickety and unreadable. What should I do? Jack, where are you? "React!" he'd say. "Go home!" I said. The fawn didn't move. I turned to look at May. She was smiling at the fawn as she smiled at everything – knowingly, sweetly. I looked in the rearview mirror. The road was dark. Nothing was coming.

When I looked at the deer again, it was looking over its shoulder at me. The expression in its eyes was perhaps resignation and terror, perhaps less. It looked and looked at me, but it didn't move. I looked into the grove beside the river for more of them or for the answer, but I could see nothing there; it was too dark. As I started to get out of the car to push the deer off the road, I saw that a car was coming towards us in the other lane, the same lane that the deer was in. "Get!" I yelled at the deer. "Shoo!" I pulled the car ahead. The deer followed me with its eyes. May smiled. I looked at the deer. I looked ahead. The headlights were coming fast and then the car hit the deer, there was glass in the air, and, then, the deer lay in a heap on the road behind my car, such a long way back, it seemed.

CHAPTER 3

The Farm Sale

The last time I drove along the Rock River I was twenty-two years old and I had just graduated from college up in Minnesota – St. Elizabeth's, a small Catholic school nobody's ever heard of. I drove all night with all my clothes and books and records in the back seat and trunk of my Mustang from Duluth down to Half Moon, not because I was in such a big hurry to see the farm or my mother or father, but because I had the romantic notion that it would be wonderful to be driving along the Rock River when the sun came up. It *was* wonderful. The dew was so heavy that every leaf and blade and spider web was encased in silver or gold, the grasses and weeds were lush, and the Rock was what I thought rivers ought to be – wide and placid and thick and brown, bounded in mud, closer to the element of earth than of sky. I had been dazzled by clear northern rivers, full of light and rocks and spray and speed, but I was at home beside this brown river that flowed between grasses and fields. While I had lived up north, I had felt I was living at the edge of something; when the sky was a particular high, thin blue, I felt that not much further north was the real north, and nearby were the vast, cold lakes. Now, where the rivers were substantial and where the heavy air pressed on me and supported me, I was near the center and at home. I drove slowly along Route 2 with the windows down feeling the thick air pass over my face, wanting to remember every dazzling plant and slant of light.

I knew I was going home for the last time to the farm where I grew up, where I had lived as a girl with my dad and grand-parents after my mother left us when I was ten and moved back in town. The farm was to be sold and the auction of household goods and farm equipment was a week away. I was being very adult about the whole thing. Not only was Dad almost sixty now, but he must have been very lonely there since Mom had divorced him. Besides, nobody was making much money at farm-ing, and that land never really belonged to us anyway. How can land belong to any one person? What can pieces of paper have to do with the land? The land would always be there for me, and so would more glamorous places than a flat-land grain farm in cen-tral Illinois. I was being very reasonable, very mature, so I was a little surprised on that drive when I would find myself suddenly crying. I was tired though; I had driven all night.

I was so tired when I got within a mile of home that I thought at first I was hallucinating all the cars and trucks that lined both sides of our road for a half mile in either direction from the house. Trucks and vans filled the side yard, and a barricade kept me from turning into my own driveway. Obviously the farm sale was this Saturday, not next Saturday. I had gotten the date mixed up – something I frequently did in those days. I couldn't even find a place to double park so I could look for Dad to tell me where to put my car.

I had to park almost half a mile away on the road and walk back toward the house. It was hard walking on gravel or grass in those high wedgie sandals I was wearing. My ankles wobbled, and my soles stuck to the soft hot asphalt, so several times I had to hop over to lean on a pickup to put a sandal back on. I remember my tight jeans were hot, but my new pink tank top was cool. I was trying out not wearing a bra, and I didn't know if I did or did not want to see someone I knew. I hoped nobody would react in a redneck way to my liberated choice about underwear. I wasn't very sure of myself; I was alternately concave and convex.

I noticed that some of the trucks and vans belonged to antique dealers. They are on to us, I thought, and I was embarrassed again for the Checks. The Checks were known to have never thrown out a thing. They were the opposite of the Flahertys, my mother's family. Flahertys were ready to pick up and move, travel light; if they didn't use it, they threw it out or sold it. My dad had raised me on that farm so I had lapses and sympathies with the Checks, but I counted myself a Flaherty. All the Flahertys held on to was land and real estate. As a matter of fact, though I called it my father's farm because he had farmed it all his life and because his grandfather had been the first to plow the land, the land, when it had belonged to any white person, had first belonged to my mother's family. They had also founded Half Moon where my mother had lived and worked at Knacker Packing since I was ten. It was Mom's Aunt Polly who was selling the farm.

In the front yard, household goods were piled up on long folding tables that must have been borrowed from the Methodist church. Though it was still early, people were browsing over boxes of magazines, piles of clothes, stacks of dishes and pots and pans. There was the old clothespin bag that Grandma had used and the clothespins. There were the laundry baskets, the old electric mixer, and the slightly melted, red plastic radio we listened to in the kitchen when I was a girl. There were cardboard boxes of old dresses, my grandmother's and grandfather's clothes. The bureaus from the bedrooms were out on the grass, and the dressing tables and beds. On one bureau was a box of old white gloves. On another, the bag of soft rags my grandmother used for dusting the good furniture. A box of corsets and girdles. Grandma's baking pans. The good dishes. A jumble of shoes and collars. The cake dish. This was awful. Where was my dad?

In the back lot, behind concession stands and the auctioneer's truck were all the plows the Checks had ever owned, and all the cultivators, planters, disks, harrows, the combines and corn pickers and tractors and wagons. Here were tools: hammers, chisels, saws, kegs of nails, and coffee cans full of little, saved, rusty parts of machinery. There was old milking equipment and harness and work gloves; twine and wire and boxes of dried-up tubes of glue; boxes and cartons of pieces of things I knew that only men could classify, but they were familiar things, and they'd always been here. The machine sheds and the falling-down barn and the corn crib were empty, and my voice calling Dad in each of them made an unfamiliar and awful sound.

Back at the house a few of the browsing people recognized me and said, "Hello, Janet" with the same tone in their voices that I'd heard at funerals. I don't know how long I walked dazed among these displays of the contents of Check barns, sheds, drawers, closets, cellars, and the attics of my childhood. People I didn't know were picking things up and turning them over: "What was this old thing, Myra?" and "I wonder why they saved this." I realized I was on the verge of losing everything.

I finally found Dad in the back yard near one of the concession stands.

"Dad, you've got to stop this. Get all these people out of here!"

"I can't do that, Janet. Don't be so dumb!"

In those wedgies I was a little taller than my father who is also a small person. This new angle felt strange.

"Janet, what are you doing here in your underwear? Go in the house and put on a shirt."

"A lot of girls don't wear bras now, Dad. Bras are so. . . "

"I didn't say anything about underwear you *weren't* wearing. I'm talking about that pink undershirt. You don't need to wear a bra." I smelled liquor on Dad's breath. He was very tense and slightly hysterical. He put his arms around me and squeezed my shoulders and threw his head back and laughed.

I'm sure my face was beet red. Who was he to comment on whether I did or didn't need a bra? I was torn between lashing out at this old man and crossing my arms. I crossed my arms and then I started crying and then I really didn't know what to do with my arms. I stood there in the yard under the box elder crying behind the concession stand where my swing set used to be, trying to stop myself from crying. I was trying to cover my face with my hands and keep my elbows close together to cover my breasts, such as they were, but I couldn't stop the rough sounds of my sobbing.

"Come on, Janet, you sound like a dog coughing corn shucks." Dad was using one of his colorful country expressions. "People will hear you. Go in the house and put on a shirt."

"The house is full of strangers," I wailed. "Dad, please, that's all our stuff. People are fingering all our stuff and Grandma and Granddad's stuff. Please, it's so awful. Can't you stop them?"

An anger I haven't seen very often happened behind Dad's

eyes and he roughly grabbed one of my now wet wrists. He jerked at my arm until my eyes were at the same level as his, until I no longer looked down at him. "Don't you know I never could stop anything in this family. Don't you have any idea yet... , have you ever thought once about what it was like for me to always be a tenant farmer on your mother's family's land? Your mother could stop this. I could just raise a little embarrassing hell, but a selfish little dumb bitch like you wouldn't know that would you? Would you?" He jerked at my arm until it hurt.

I just looked at him and I remember thinking, he doesn't mean this; he's just upset. He's drunk, maybe. My mouth must have quivered like a baby's. My ankles wobbled. My arm hurt. My face was wet with tears and snot. I was a mess. Dad looked hard at me for a few moments, then the anger went out of his face and he laughed.

"Sit down right here." And he twisted my arm so I sat down on the grass in the shade of the concession truck, in the racket of a condenser, while he went around front, got some paper napkins and a cup of water. He sat down in front of me and dipped a napkin in the water and squeezed it out. With this dough-like wad he washed my face, and then he dried it with another napkin. "Stay right here," he said and disappeared into the house. Even from here and over the sound of the condenser, I could hear when he ran up the stairs that there was no carpet on them and that the upstairs rooms were empty. I started to cry again; I was crying in my hands when Dad came back out and, standing beside me and walking around me, took my hands one at a time and put them through the sleeves of one of his faded brown plaid shirts.

"Now I'm going to get you something to eat. Do you still forget to eat, then get grouchy as hell? Janet? Do you?" Squatting down in front of me, he was trying to get his fingers between the heels of my hands, so he could get me to look at him. "Did you eat today, Janet?"

Finally I shook my head no and began to quiet down.

"Great, then I'll get you something. Stay here now." In a minute or so, Dad was back with a paper tray of four hot dogs and two cups of coffee.

"Four hot dogs?" I asked.

"They're small. Two for you and two for me. Pinch off the extra bread at the ends and throw it under the truck." I did as I was told. We ate the hot dogs; both of us were starved.

As we sat in the shade and ate and drank the sweet coffee with milk, I think we both recognized something of ourselves in the other — the same hunger, the same silence, the same irresistible optimism after eating. We ate and we watched the legs of people under the trucks and trailers that surrounded us.

"What on earth is this, Etta?" We could hear people's comments as they picked over our stuff. At the same moment both of us became afraid to overhear too much, something we could not laugh off.

Dad crumpled all the paper together. "I bet you drove all night. Is that right?"

My eyelids were heavy. A deep inhale was all the answer I could give.

"Well, no wonder! No wonder!" Dad stood up and put his hands like a cap on my hair. "I saw Carl Hawn here a little while ago. I bet Shirley's here too. I'll get one of them to take you over to their place where you can sleep and then when this is all over, I'll come get you around supper time. OK?"

We could both hear someone asking where Ed Check was. "Anybody seen Ed Check? Ed Check. Short little bow-legged guy with eight or nine grey hairs?"

"OK, Dad. I'll go over to the Hawns."

"Wait right here. I'll be right back."

I could hear them find him. "Ed, there you are. What the hell kind of host are you? Give a big party like this and then just disappear. People have questions, Ed. You gotta answer the people's questions."

"Not dumb ones though. You ought to know that, Lyle."

I could hear him disappear from me. I could hear the murmur of voices, the drone of the auctioneer near the machine shed, the breeze in the box elder, the condenser. The grass was soft and cool and I could do nothing but lie down on my stomach and, with my face on my arms, go to sleep.

I woke up when something nudged my elbow. I opened my eyes. A big work shoe. A big foot was right beside my elbow. I looked up.

"Hi, Carl."

"Hi, Janet. Your dad says you want to go over to our place and get out of all this."

This seemed familiar, looking at Carl like this. I remembered that when we were kids he used to throw me to the ground and then put his foot on my arm to keep me from getting up. Carl was only two years older than I was, but he and Shirley had had to get married at 17, and now he looked like a middle-aged farmer and I was a college kid.

"It was Dad's idea. That I go over there and get some sleep. I drove all night."

"If you don't want to, I won't take you." Carl was always quick to perceive offense. He backed up when I sat up.

"I want to. I want to get away from all this. And I'd like to see Shirley and the kids."

"Shirley's not there right now. I'll just take you over and come back."

I stood up and followed Carl to the back of the place and he guided me through the crowd as if this were not the place that I knew better than any place on earth. Carl's pickup was behind the machine shed in the tall grass. Just before I got to the truck I stepped into a hidden depression a foot below the level of the grass and I fell to my knees. "A hole!" I said.

"Sure, it's a hole!" Carl sounded less like a middle-aged man. His voice was affectionate. "Don't you remember? That's where we, you and me and Jack and Joyce were going to build a hideout, don't you remember? That's the foundation hole of hideout number fifty or sixty." Carl was laughing.

I was still on my knees in the tall grass. "It's still here? It's still here?" My voice was beginning to quiver again.

Carl got in the truck and pushed open the door on my side. I got in, wiping my eyes. "Oh jeez," I sighed. I tried to keep from crying again while we headed out through the lot, bouncing in the truck. Carl didn't notice.

"You know who owns all this now, don't you?" he asked me.

"No. Nobody told me," I said.

"I do."

"You do?" I reached over and grabbed Carl's forearm with both of my hands. "Oh, Carl, that's great. I'm so glad." I began to cry one more time, the last time that day. This time Carl noticed and I don't think he minded. He liked it too when I said, "It won't go to a stranger. It'll stay in the family, almost."

"Watch it, kid. Don't jerk my driving arm or you'll kill us both and Shirley'll own the place and then where will we be!"

The Hawns and the Checks were almost family. My best friend all the way through school, even though she was a year younger, was Joyce. And for years I had gone steady with Jack who was three years older than I. It was only in the last five years, when Jack and I had broken up, and he had been going with a girl named Donna, that I had lost track of the Hawns.

Now I didn't know where Jack was and I didn't know where Joyce was.

"Jack's up in Madison," Carl said. "He's working for a professor and going to school again. Another degree in farming."

"Ag, Carl!"

"I suppose. Isn't it funny that the one person who always had all the answers is still going to school?"

"Are he and Donna . . . ?"

"Split? Split. They split for good."

We were bumping along the little two-track road through the fields. At the center of the square mile, which now all belonged to Carl, was the corn crib, and crossing diagonally from the corners of the farm, the drainage ditch. We bounced around the crib and over the rickety bridge.

Sitting high in the truck, with grassheads bumping the front of the truck and the crickets like a machine out the windows, I began to feel wonderful. Jack was not going with that girl anymore and Carl had bought my family's farm. Though the artifacts of my past were being picked over by strangers and carried all over the country, there was still Dad, and Carl would keep the land, and there was Jack. Maybe he was waiting for me, as I, at that moment, was beginning to wait for him. Jack! My shoulders relaxed and I felt thin and light and happy next to Carl in this same truck that the Hawns had used for driving across the field to the Checks' for probably twenty-five years.

"Does the door still fly open when you go around corners?"

"Sure. Want to see?"

By then we were at Carl's place. "Get away from that door and hang on."

I slid over next to Carl and put my arm around his shoulders. Around and around the oil shed he drove faster and faster until the door flew open and the dust came rolling in and he pulled up in the gravel drive, slamming on the brakes, skidding nearly to the fence, and the door slammed shut again.

"I must be getting into my second childhood," said Carl as he leaned over me to open the door so I could get out. Carl smelled just like he did when he was a boy. Joyce and I used to compare Jack and Carl, and though they in many ways smelled alike, we decided that Carl smelled more like an animal and Jack smelled more like a cornfield. The smell of Carl. I loved that smell. My eyes were closed. I was ten years old.

Carl nudged me. "Nobody's home. Shirley and the kids are at her mom's. They won't be home till ten or so tonight. So just go on in there and make yourself at home. Lie down anyplace and go to sleep. You look like you need it, kid." Carl laughed and pushed me out of the truck, then he drove off more sedately, more like the middle-aged farmer he was becoming.

I felt light and clean. Ready for anything. The breeze on my face reminded me . . . that I was alive? That I had escaped this brush with . . . what? I had not been giving a thought to the things that meant the most to me, my father, the farm, and Jack who I began to think I'd always loved. I had not thought about them and I had almost lost them. Now I had another chance.

The breeze and the sun on my face and at the back of my neck seemed to be erasing the borders between me and the perfect summer day. I wanted to run in it, swallow it, enclose it all in my arms, but I stood there on the Hawn's walk watching the dust from Carl's truck rise above the road, recede. I didn't notice at the time, but my hand was slow to release to the air the feel of Carl's shoulder. My right hand remembered the bones of his wrist; my left hand his sun-warmed back.

I turned and, leaning on the gate, took off my sandals, walked up to the house, taking care to avoid the chicken crap on the walk. The Hawns had always had chickens, long after everyone else had given up on them. So where most farmers had spirea, petunias, and grass, the Hawns had spirea, dust nests, and dirt. The yard was the same as it always had been, though here and there Shirley's attempts at more elegant flowers – peonies and rosebushes – weren't doing too well.

Carl had put in cement steps instead of the wooden ones, but the back porch was the same. Translucent plastic on the windows flapped back and forth in the breeze and the grey painted floor was covered with the same kind of debris of ten and twenty years ago – muddy boots, bags of chicken feed, oily jackets, caps, tricycles, and buckets of muddy carrots from the garden. In the dim kitchen, the hum was the same and the smell was the same, though maybe there was less gravy in the smell than when Nelda was cooking here years ago. The dining-room table was neatly stacked with bills and checks and mail. In the living room were the same low grey-brown sofa and matching chairs Nelda bought in the fifties.

When I went upstairs, I was getting in deeper. I was going back in time. This was a pocket of air from my childhood. Trapped under the roof of this house, which was as familiar to me as my own house, was this air, these smells, this gift given to me undeserved. I felt that I had come back solidly and wholly to a place and to the people who were home; I was sure the feeling would last. I resolved never again to be so careless as I had been for the last four years.

Though the mother and the father here were no longer Nelda and D.E., but Carl and Shirley, the mother and father's room was the same. On the windows were the same beige drapes and sheers and Venetian blinds from the fifties. The dark varnished arch of the bedboard and the matching dresser and dressing table were all in the same places. The bedspread was still white chenille, though the beige wallpaper was new. There was a pair of blue rag rugs on the floor, but there were no ornaments be-

sides Shirley and Carl's wedding photograph in a big oak frame
and a studio picture of the two oldest children in front of a scrim
of a romantic forest. The children, the older girl and the little
boy, were holding hands and smiling like Hansel and Gretel setting out. I looked for signs of Shirley in the room, but other than
the wedding picture, a bathrobe hanging on the back of the door,
and a pink shell dish of pins and earrings and change, there was
none. I thought I'm as much at home here as Shirley, yet when I
opened the closet door, I was disturbed by the mingled scents of
a man and a woman.

The girl's room was nothing like mine was when I was a girl
and it was nothing like Joyce's when this was hers. This little
girl, Mandy, lived in pink and was surrounded by stuffed
animals and dolls. The bed and dresser and bureau were pink
and so were the ruffled curtains and the bedspread. Joyce and I
had both grown up in rooms of left-over furniture and boys' toys.
I didn't know this little girl, but I felt toward her the way I felt
about my older sister, a familiar resentment of her carefully
documented and decorated childhood.

The baby's room was like any baby's room, but the little boy's
room is where I stayed, where I lay down and slept. The
wallpaper was flowered; no redecorating had been done for this
little boy. The maple bed and carved-up and crayoned dresser
were the same as when Jack and Carl were boys. There was the
same jumble of boys' stuff on the old army trunk used as a bedside table. In a daze now from fatigue and from time travel, I lay
down on Carl's little boy's bed, and when my face touched the
pillow, I breathed in full-blown images of the boys Jack and
Carl. I smelled the way they smelled like everything on the farm
– the sun on dust and corn, tractor grease, the west wind,
tomato plants, farm cats, ball gloves, and grape jelly. It was all
distilled in the pillow.

For a few minutes I lay there looking out the window watching the clouds cross in a dignified manner. An airplane droned a long way away, and the breezes filtered lazily first through the soft maple trees, then the screens, then gently bowed the rain stained curtain. When I was almost asleep, I turned onto my other side and reached my fingers out to the wallpaper to peel one more tiny piece of flaking blue flower to show another tiny piece of green bird below.

I was curled up on that bedspread with bears on it when Dad gently shook my shoulder that evening. I lay there awhile and then I went downstairs.

When I came, blinking, into the kitchen light, both Carl and Dad laughed.

"Your kid's a zombie, Ed. Too bad."

I ignored this and sat down at the kitchen table, breathed through my nose, didn't talk.

They were both hilarious. Dad had just lost everything. Carl was afraid he had taken on too much. They'd been drinking, and now they were hungry.

Carl opened a can of pork and beans, poured them on a good plate, went out on the porch and, holding the door open, called, "Here kitty, kitty, kitty," Eight or nine yellow cats slipped through the door like ears of corn through a chute. Eight or nine cats looked at Carl when they sniffed the beans. Carl was laughing hysterically. The disgusted cats pulled back their lips and gingerly ate the beans one by one.

Dad was standing on a low stool in Shirley's pantry. "Carl, forget them goddamned store-bought beans. I ain't eating any store-bought beans. In here, Carl. Here's real food." He began piling jars of Shirley's home-canned goods into his arms. "Real food, made by the real hands of a real woman." Jars of tomatoes, plums, wax beans. He brought them in and set them on the kitchen table.

"That's last year's stuff," Carl said gruffly. "It might have been real once, but it ain't real any more."

"It's real, Carl. Look at that red. Taste this." Dad had a cereal bowl full of tomatoes. He poured out a bowl of tomatoes for me.

I *was* coming to. "These *are* good, Carl." Then it came to me. I put my fork down. "Have you guys been smoking dope?"

They both giggled. "Oh God," I said. "I don't believe it."

Carl was indignant. "I bet you've done it a time or two up in Minneapolis."

"Duluth."

"Whatever."

"I used to," I said, "but I outgrew it. Where'd you get it? Who would sell dope to you two?"

"In Ed's machine shed. Nobody sold it to us. Lyle Statter'd taken some off his kid he'd just beat up for smoking it. He gave it to us."

"That must have been a sight." I tried to picture Dad and Carl smoking grass in Dad's shed, but I couldn't.

"In Carl's shed," Dad said quietly.

"What?"

"It's Carl's shed, not mine."

"Whoever," said Carl. This bothered him.

We were all three sitting at the table now eating right out of the jars. Pickles, corn relish, tomatoes, green beans, wax beans.

"What are you going to do now, Dad?"

"Open a jar of plums."

"You know what I mean!" I realized that now he had no place. Where would he live? Where would I live?

"I'm moving into the hotel in town. All my stuff that I want's either already there or in my truck."

"You ought to get a real place, Ed. The hotel's for sale again.

Who knows what will happen with that."

Then Dad asked me, "Hey, Janet, what are you going to do?"
It had just occurred to him to wonder too.

I hadn't thought about it, and I had no plans, but all of a sudden I knew what I was going to do. "I'm staying here." I carefully put a whole tomato in my mouth.

"Here?" both men said at once and pointed at the kitchen floor.

I chewed a minute. "There!" I said, pointing west. "At our place."

"That's Carl's place." Dad leaned forward, enunciated as if he were talking to an idiot.

"I'm going to stay there. What do you think I came home for?"

Dad turned to Carl. "What *are* you going to do with the house?"

"Rent it."

"That's right, rent it to me."

"You don't have any money," Dad accused.

"I have some," (I had about eighty dollars) "and I'll get a job. I'll walk beans for Carl this summer."

Both men laughed and I did too. Walking beans was high-school kids' work. No one ever paid rent hoeing weeds and corn out of fields of beans.

"I don't care. Stay for a while," Carl said. "But what will you do for furniture?"

"I don't need furniture. Just a bed and a stove and refrigerator and bathroom. A washer and dryer. A table and two chairs. Sheets. Towels. Well, don't laugh. Most of that's in the house, I bet. Haven't you got a mattress and a table you were going to store?"

"Sure, Janet, we'll unload the truck tomorrow. I just wish I'd known. What a pain in the neck!" Dad hated carrying things.

"I'll help you, Ed," Carl said as car lights swept through the kitchen and we heard a car in the drive.

"There's Shirley and the kids." It was almost ten o'clock. Carl got up and held the back door open, his face now eager and tense.

Shirley came in alone, greeted Dad and me cooly, put her purse down on the counter, and got the water bottle out of the refrigerator. She had gained weight since I last saw her. Though she was only a little older than I, she looked like a middle-aged farm wife. I felt a little silly, dressed like a teen-ager.

"The kids asleep in the car?" Carl was ready to go out and get them.

"They stayed at Mom's." Shirley's voice was low, careful.

Carl didn't say anything for a minute. "Janet hasn't seen the baby."

"Some other time," said Shirley quietly.

"They're going to stay here tonight. Ed's all moved out."

"Some other time," Shirley said again. Something was wrong here. There were three long breaths drawn, then everyone watched silently while I fastened my sandals. Dad and I got up to go.

"I'll see you tomorrow," said Carl. "We'll get that stuff off the truck."

"Right," said Dad and we left.

Dad and I got rooms at the Starlite Inn on the highway after we'd rescued my dew-covered Mustang from the dark road. It was ghostly and depressing to drive that cold car away from our dark and empty house. I shivered all the way to the motel though I rolled up the windows and turned up the radio.

The next morning Dad and I unloaded two single mattresses, a little dresser, and a table and four chairs. That's all I wanted.

Carl didn't show up. With few words, Dad left for town. "Don't forget, your old dad's only eight miles away."

"I won't, Dad. I'll take you out to eat with my bean money."

"Don't forget to eat, Janet." I watched Dad drive away without looking back at the land his grandfather had broken with one of John Deere's first plows.

CHAPTER 4

The Houses

When Dad drove off that morning and left me there alone on the farm for the first time, I remember saying out loud, "Now you can be anyone you want." First I unloaded my stereo and books and records and stuff from the trunk of the Mustang, then I unpacked and cleaned up the house. During the next few weeks, I tried out ways to be.

Sometimes in the mornings, I stacked Joan Baez and Ian and Sylvia records on my stereo and, wearing a long Indian print skirt, I swept and scrubbed the bare and echoing rooms. Neither Carl nor Dad had bothered to have the phone or any of the utilities disconnected. The curtains were still there and I collected odd pieces of furniture – leftover from the sale – from all over the house and farm. I washed the curtains and carried them out in a bushel basket to the clothesline. When I rehung the clean, dry curtains and the coarse cloth touched my face, I was my

Grandmother Check, I was a farmer's wife and I thought of Jack.

In the evenings I lit the candles – I'd forgotten to ask Dad for lamps – and I played Dave Brubeck albums I hadn't returned to JoAnn, and drank black coffee. My Bohemian living room suited me at night – Indian print bedspread and pillows on a mattress on the floor, books piled on a board-and-brick bookshelf, album covers scattered around the room. Sometimes I tried to smoke as I declaimed – in English – lines out of my Penguin anthology of French verse, especially the good parts of Oscar Milosz's long love poem to his childhood house: "House of the beautiful dark summers of my childhood, . . . you who knew so well how to hide me from cruel glances, O accomplice, gentle accomplice! . . . I have breathed many souls, but none had that good smell of fresh table-linen and golden bread and old windows open to June's bees. . . . Why did I not live alone without desire beneath your low ceilings? . . . Why did you let me leave? . . . Your hair smells of summer, the moon and the earth. We must live, live, do nothing but live."

It was in the evenings that I missed my friends from college. I imagined them visiting me: I would show them around the farm and tell them witty stories about what had happened here, and we'd stay up all night listening to jazz and reading French poetry. But I didn't write to them and I didn't call.

Sometimes I just got up and put on some old shorts and a halter top and wandered around the lots and outbuildings and listened to the sound of my footfalls in those empty buildings. I luxuriated in all that space that was mine now. And I collected details. I knew how many fat black-and-yellow garden spiders had woven their webs across paths. I knew where the cock pheasant came out of the cornfield every morning. I knew where the rabbits' nests were, knew that two crippled pigeons lived in the old corn crib. It seemed funny to have this information and not be able to tell Joyce or Jack or Carl. I called Carl and Shirley's now and then, but I never caught them at home.

Like most of the Checks, I was fairly successful at putting money worries out of my mind. I guess I assumed that Carl was not serious about collecting rent from me. I assumed I would not starve to death.

One afternoon out in the weeds I found the old wobbly blue table that used to be on our back porch. Nobody had wanted to buy it. As I dragged it up to the house, I could hear Granddad Orin's telescope rattling in the table's drawer where it had always been kept. Later I found the blue chair in the cellar. Now, with the table and the chair and the telescope in their proper places, I could, if I wanted to, sit in the chair with my feet on the porch rail, lean back, clear a window in the Virginia creeper vines, and, like my dad and my grandfather before me, spy on the Hawns.

Now and then, I looked for work in a desultory way. After I drank several cups of coffee sitting in the blue chair on the back porch, watching the fields heat up and the grass grow tall around the house, I would drive into Bloomington wearing my job interview dress and high heels and stockings. I hated to write letters and make phone calls, so I just showed up at office after office where puzzled or indifferent or hostile secretaries told me there was nothing available and it wouldn't do me any good to see Mr. So-and-So. I had a college degree in French; I wanted an interesting job, but I couldn't type, so there was nothing I was qualified to do. I was waiting for Jack. He would come home sooner or later.

My mother worked in a small packing house in Half Moon. I wasn't sure what she did, but I knew that she had a lot of friends there, most of them male. She was famous for being a little bit raunchy in her talk, fiercely Democratic in a Republican town, and an active, Irish, underdog Catholic in a town of tee-totaling Methodists and Baptists. Two Sundays in a row, Mom and my sister Mary drove out after Mass to see me. They brought each time a bag of donuts, slips of paper with the names and phone numbers of job contacts, and plenty of free advice. Mom could not understand why I didn't have more "get-up-and-go," and Mary, who didn't have much either, could not understand why I hadn't got up and went. She couldn't see why a person like me would think she could be single and happy in this part of the country, which either meant that Mary and I were not at all alike or that she – divorced from that jerk Jim Starr and living alone also in this part of the country – was very unhappy. Mary, who was thirteen years older than I, had married young, been deserted by Jim Starr, and now lived like an old lady in town in a tiny house on the meagerest of incomes from some property in town left to her by Grandmother Flaherty. I hadn't even been thought of when Grandmother Flaherty died, so I wasn't in on that. Though I hated to ask, I borrowed some money from Mom. Mom and Mary and I sat in the yard both Sundays and drank coffee and ate donuts while they gave me advice and looked around them and told me how much they did not miss this place. After the second Sunday, they said they weren't coming back here because it was too depressing, and if I wanted to see them, I had to go in town. Then they stood up, smoothed their skirts, and left. I was waiting for Jack.

After I'd been there about two weeks, I drove over to Carl and Shirley's one night after supper. I hadn't seen them except for that first day, the day of the sale. When I pulled in the driveway, Carl was standing on the top back-porch step. I got out of the car and walked up toward the house and said hello to Carl, but he just stood there – barefooted, in jeans and tee shirt, beer in hand – and didn't speak. I was a little uneasy until he smiled and then said, "Have a seat out here. Shirley's putting the kids to bed." Then Carl pointed at one of the steps and sat down. So did I. As soon as he did, his face changed back to the same inward look it had before he smiled, the way it must have looked before I got there. Both of us sat there silent for a few moments and listened to splashing and little children's squeals and Shirley's sharp reprimands coming from the upstairs bathroom above us. I realized that Carl had been standing there before I came, listening to his children's squeals poke out at the silence of the fields. I got the idea he did this every night.

When the children's ruckus receded to the bedrooms at the front of the house, Carl stood up and came down the steps, loose-legged, watching for the chicken crap on the walk. Next to the weed-overgrown wire fence, he righted a rusted green metal lawn chair, one we played in as children. When he turned it over, rusty water poured off, but he sat down in it, putting one of his long bare feet on the seat up next to his butt; the other leg he stretched out into the yard. Carl then looked up at me as if he'd just remembered I was there and said, "Oh, go on in to the refrigerator and get yourself a beer if you want. If you're old enough. Get me one, too." He smiled. I didn't like beer much, but I went in and got us each one and came back out and sat down backwards on one of the children's tricycles parked near Carl. There was no place else, unless I wanted to sit in chicken shit on the grass or shout at Carl from the back step.

We sat like that for a while, me on the tricycle, Carl listening with his face in the darkness and his feet and hands in the blue-white light of the pole light. The sounds of the children going to bed floated down to us in the dim yard like tatters of pastel cloth. As I listened and as I watched Carl listen, I became sure of two things: I have no idea what goes on in Carl Hawn's mind; and he has never given any thought to his hands and his feet. They were very nice to look at, but I bet Carl didn't know that. Both were long and thin, but his hands were dark and his feet very light. I knew that they would feel very different from each other

– his hands, warm, dry, dusty; his feet, cool, smooth, bony, and damp.

I had never really looked at Carl before. It was always Jack I had looked at. Because Carl's face is so triangular, almost Asian, one time when we were kids on the school bus a little kid asked Joyce how come her brother Carl was Chinese when Jack was an American. As I sat there looking at Carl's feet, I remembered one time when Joyce had said that faces weren't everything, and why don't I pay attention to Carl because he has beautiful hands and feet while Jack's were gnarled up and stunted looking things. "And it will only get worse," she said. I wondered where Joyce was. I came to hear about Jack, and this was a good way to lead up to it. "Where's Joyce, now?" I asked Carl.

His face was still in deep shadow and his hands were clasped around his legs. For a minute I thought he hadn't heard me. "Where's Joyce, Carl?"

Carl, who'd been leaning back toward the front yard, leaned forward with a start, put his bare feet on the ground and his elbows on his knees. He rested his face in his hands and rubbed his eyes as if he were waking up.

"Joyce?" he asked, the words muffled by his hands, and then there was another long pause. He raised his face out of his hands and looked at me. One of the border collies, his tags clinking, appeared from the dark under the porch and came over to Carl where it leaned against his legs. Carl didn't seem to notice the dog, though his hands petted it. "She's still with that church group, as far as I know. We don't see much of her, and she doesn't seem much like herself when we do. I suppose she'll get over all that one of these days."

As he talked, I saw myself and Joyce as nine-year-olds standing toe deep in the soft, tractor-greased dust in the lot or standing in tall weeds busy being short or crawling in the grass watching the ants rise up against us. I called up detail, piece by piece, in some wrong order: the hot sun on our dry and dusty arms; we wore seersucker shorts and no shirts; sticky, ugly feet; hands clasped, palms wet, me absent-mindedly flicking the wart on her thumb; the smell of the sun on our unwashed heads; we were unsavory little girls with black fingernails. Everything not nailed down we turned over; we put everything in our hands, made all stuff our business. We ambled around and bickered and lied and spent most of our days deciding what to play or trying to decide whose turn it was to decide what to play or making up the rules for the game we were getting ready to play or casting the game or rigging up the costumes or constructing the setting. We hardly ever got down to it, whatever it would have been.

And I saw a very clear, strange picture in my mind of Joyce when she and I were about seven. It was night and I was standing in the dark in the Hawn's yard. The back-porch light was shining down on Joyce standing on the walk beside the house. She was wearing a long sleeveless nightgown and her feet were bare. The yellow porch light shined down on her curly, silvery hair, on her brown face, on her brown arms which were smooth and beautifully formed. She was singing, holding her arms away from her body with her palms forward in an almost ceremonial gesture. She was singing to all the cats who were gathered there for their supper. Some of the cats were eating out of the old skillet which was their dish, some looked up at her, and some of them watched her as I did, from outside the light. I wished I could remember what Joyce was singing to those cats.

I also wished that Joyce was the same Joyce, but Dad had told me that one day two women came to his door to tell him about Jesus and the end of the world, and it was only halfway through their spiel that he realized that one of those hard-faced women was Joyce Hawn whom he had known since she was a baby. I didn't want to know that Joyce. I didn't want to have to make the connection between the old Joyce and the new one.

"Tell me about Jack," I said to Carl.

"I wish the baby wasn't asleep. I'd like you to see her. You know we named her 'Nellie' sort of after Mom. Shirley wouldn't hear of 'Nelda.' 'Nellie' is close. I like 'Nellie.' " Carl was listening to himself say "Nellie."

I listened too. Something was wrong, but I didn't know what. There were allegiances here I didn't understand. Where was Jack? If Jack were here there would be no guessing about what was going on. Jack would tell you, and, though you might resist because Jack is so uncool, you don't in the end resist Jack's version of events and what Jack wants because of the force of his energy and concentration and generosity and organization – Jack's will. Being with Jack solves a lot of problems, I remembered, because Jack was always in charge. He had always figured out what to do, where to go, how to get there. All the next steps in his life and the lives of those who didn't resist were visible in front of you. I felt very unsure of myself here with Carl, and I missed Jack's open and kind face, his optimism and gentleness; for the first time that summer I missed the real Jack, not just the idea of Jack. No one in my whole life had ever taken better care of me than Jack; even as a teen-ager, he was solicitous and considerate.

"Do you hear from Jack?" I tried again.

"Three or four times a year." Carl was silent a moment. "He comes down at Christmas and Thanksgiving and a couple of other times. I guess he's working his rear off to put himself through school, but he doesn't have too much more to go – a semester or two." Carl was impatient, whether with me or with Jack or with talking about Jack, I couldn't tell. "Wait here a minute," he said and ran past me into the house. He came back in a minute and stood in front of me. He had slipped thongs onto his feet. He reached down for my hand and pulled me to my feet. Then he thrust a piece of paper into my hand as he pushed me toward my car. "Jack's phone number," he said. Carl had his arm tight around my shoulders and was walking me a bit roughly to my car. "Go call him." His voice was hoarse and urgent. "Get all this over with. Donna was a mistake and you thought there might be somebody more 'glamorous' than Jack; is that it?" He was both pulling me and pushing me down the sidewalk toward my car in the darkness under the big maple tree. I realized only then that Carl was drunk. "Go call him. Go home and call Jack." One hand was rough on my arm and the other tight and gentle on my shoulders. When we got to the car, I couldn't see him, it was so dark, but with his body he pressed me against my car so I couldn't open the door. He leaned against me, his back to the light and I could see nothing of his face. His dry hands moved up and down my arms. He smelled like sweat and beer. "Go home and call Jack," he whispered with some fierceness in his voice. "Call him tonight, will you? Will you call him?" I could see only darkness and feel only Carl, and now I had no answer for him. I didn't know what I would do. I wanted to stay with him; I didn't want to go home and call his brother. He held my head to his chest. My ear was pressed to his chest so that I heard his strong heart and three long breaths. "I'll call him," I said, but my voice gave me away.

I went home and thumbtacked the number on the wall next to the phone. Jack's phone number in Carl's handwriting.

CHAPTER 5

The Near Occasion

Two weeks later I hadn't called Jack and I had stopped looking for work. I didn't know what I would do about a job, but I was beginning to see why I had come home to the farm. I vaguely wanted to make some connection here, though I didn't know with what. I just knew, even then, that everything I truly knew, I had learned there on the farm. Since I had left for school, I had stopped learning with my body; I had stopped hearing stories. I wasn't finished with this house and these fields, with these farmers. I had spent most of my life among them waiting for my life to begin, and I wanted it to begin here; I wanted to set out from here.

I stayed home. No one drove down our road. In the mornings in my nightgown, I walked barefooted all around the yard and the lot, drinking coffee which I had recently begun to like.

Grass was wet on my legs, the soft dust in the lot muddied my feet and dried there, and breezes were nice under my night-gown. I sat in the sun on the back step and leaned against the warm clapboards. Pheasants called from inside the cornfields, crows called from above them, and doves mourned on the wires.

In the house I wandered from room to room daydreaming Jack home, daydreaming a life for us there in that house, but not a life with furniture, not a life in which we had to mow the lawn. Upstairs, I carried a blanket and pillow from room to empty room. I read and took naps in each room, and I memorized the various views of fields from each window. Each day the house became more and more my house as I watched the progress of light through each empty room and listened to the house creak as it heated and cooled, adjusted and settled. I thought about Jack in each of the rooms, but, because I wanted to live like this and because the real Jack would have things for us to do, I pic-tured us – farmer and farm wife – doing together only what I was doing alone – eating and sleeping and looking. I didn't imagine us talking to each other, but it was difficult to imagine Jack not talking. The only expression that I could dream on his face that would make him be quiet was puzzlement, so in all my daydreams, Jack looked at me quizzically and I led him by the hand.

Though Jack and I had gone steady for more than three years in high school and just after, we had never made love. Jack al-ways said he was too close to my dad for that; he wanted to be able to look my dad in the eye. This drove me crazy, but every time Jack brought me home and we would say goodnight, then, after I went upstairs, he and Dad would sit on the back porch just below my bedroom and I would listen to them quietly talk-ing. Jack sounded like a grown man and I was so proud of him. I loved to lie awake and listen to them talk in the dark below me.

I was proud of Jack, but I was also seventeen years old and I was tired of this careful and solicitous man; I was sick of Jack's plaid, short-sleeved shirts and his chinos with tabs. Jack was so predictable and so good that I ran away for a week with my crazy friend Marcie and two guys from Peoria who wore black and rode motorcycles. I told Mom and Dad where I was, but I shouldn't have. Everyone was furious, so furious, that it took some of them years to get over it. It turned out that everybody — Mom, Dad, Jack, Carl, Joyce, and even their parents, D.E. and Nelda — had big plans that were based on me being good and marrying Jack. Jack thought that he and I would eventually farm both the Flaherty and Hawn halves of the section and we'd live happily ever after. Dad saw himself living to be an old man in this house where he was born, with me and Jack and his grandchildren a mile away. Mom saw her daughter married to "a good man and a provider"; she'd "never have to worry about me again." Joyce saw her best friend becoming her sister. D.E. and Nelda could retire and leave their farm in the hands of their *good* boy, Jack, and not Carl, the bad one who had gotten Shirley Chase pregnant in their last year of high school. My sin was against so many people and so public that even Jack couldn't forgive me, so we broke up and the future of everyone had to be rearranged. Jack, who had been living at home and driving into the university several nights a week, decided to go to ag school full time before he settled down to farm for the rest of his life. D.E. and Nelda retired and, temporarily, let Carl and Shirley and their little baby move into the farm house until Jack should want it and Carl, who didn't want to farm then, found something else. It went on and on. I had never dreamed how far waves could go out from one impulsive act and I was amazed at how much I missed Jack at first.

Now here I was, five years later, trying to dream a reasonable, sweet dream of Jack again, but now and then, walking around those empty rooms, up to my neck in the tepid, thick Illinois summer, I would be almost lifted off my feet when an image of Carl moved me like a swell in the ocean.

One night I dreamed I was making love to one of the Hawns; this dream man smelled like both Jack and Carl. He was on top of me, inside of me, and his face was in the dark. So, in the dream, I reached out with my fingers to feel whose hands they were, but this dream man's arms grew and grew out of my reach so I couldn't feel his hands. Then I tried to reach his feet with mine so I could tell which of them it was, but his legs grew out of my reach. I woke up hot and scared and that day I began to spy on the Hawns.

As soon as I got up that morning, I made coffee and took it out on the porch, and I took the telescope out of the drawer in the blue table. That telescope, which was so powerful you could count the nails in a corncrib two miles away, had belonged to my grandfather Orin, the first of the "lazy" Checks. The story goes that Orin sat right there where I was sitting and, too lazy to walk or drive out to the fields, looked through the spyglass to check on his crops. When I aimed the spyglass out across the fields I saw what he must have seen, fields of crops, and bored with that as he must have been, I then aimed it at the only thing to see besides bugs and heat and crops and clouds – the Hawns. I realized then that voyeurism must be another of the Check vices and I wonder if lust was a Check vice or did I get it from the Flahertys.

I settled into the chair, put my feet up on the porch rail, rested the spyglass between my knees, and focused on the Hawns' place.

It was still early morning and very quiet. Nothing was up over there but a yellow cat walking across the powdery dust in the lot. The trees were still. The chickens were in the dust under the bushes. I looked at all the west windows of the Hawns' house and saw no movement, no face or arm. The cars were gone or in the shed. I wanted to see Carl and Shirley. I didn't want to see them in bed or anything like that. Besides, their bedroom is on the other side of the house. I wanted to see two people talk and do in the daytime whatever they do when they sleep in the same bed each night. How could they, in the daytime, keep their hands off each other? Over and over I imagined in their dark bedroom a circle of light in which I saw Carl's brown hand on a woman's white hip. How could they get out of bed in the mornings? How could they not blush in front of the children? Their life together, I could see from a distance, was made out of nothing I had, nothing I knew anything about. I wanted to see how married people lived their lives, how they got along. How do people love each other when they're used to each other? What do men and women do besides fight and make love and not speak to each other?

I thought of my grandfather, Orin, unhappily married to Grandma, a big, soft woman who spent her life from about age forty to sixty in bed in the darkened northwest bedroom full of dark furniture and green brocade. She, as the old people said, just took to her bed. Then when Granddad got so sick, she got up and took care of him as if she had not spent the last twenty years in bed being waited on. Why did she go to bed and why did she get up? Why did my mother stay here as long as she had and why did she leave? Though my eye was focused on the Hawns' place, what I was seeing were the Checks and their unhappy marriages in the house at my back. I tried to focus on something other than the past which still seemed to be going on in the house behind me, but I didn't want to think about the tense marriage of Carl and Shirley and I didn't want to think about Jack and I didn't want to think about Carl. I focused the spyglass on the chicory because nothing I was dwelling on was good for me.

If your eye just rested long enough on the right small thing, I thought, a flower, a bright beetle, an innocent bystander like a leaf on a stem, you could get everything you needed through your eye. I tried to look at the chicory flowers by the Hawns' driveway, but that color, that soft blue with lavender and grey, doesn't carry well over long distances, maybe because it is the color of distance itself. Chicory flowers don't seem anchored to the earth; they float in midair. The color is thin and the plant itself is thin and spindly. When you walk up close to the chicory plant, you find the flowers so far apart on the stems that you can't get enough of the color in your eye. You can't pick chicory flowers because the stems are so tough, and even if you did, the flowers wilt in a minute, the blue disappears like colors do when fish die out of water. When the sun is bright and the sky is blue like this, you can't see both the stem and the flower at the same time. It's an optical illusion, a trick of the sun or your eyes. Where is the trick done, I wondered, inside or outside of me? I would like to learn the trick.

I remembered one day when I was a little girl of about ten, I sat here on this porch and, imitating Dad, propped my feet on the rail and the telescope on my knees like this and I watched Dad and D.E. Hawn out in the field walking beans. I remember realizing that day that you could tell things about people just from watching their bodies move around, and I remember learning then that, when you separate the bodies of human beings from their voices, the bodies can seem ridiculous to you, so you can watch them and feel superior. Children learn this easily when they watch television with the sound off. It is odd, I thought, that voiceless bodies are ridiculous, while a bodiless voice – radio, revelation, the telephone – has dignity and weight. I also remember realizing that day that I knew those two people out in the field so well that, without hearing them, I could tell what they were saying; I knew their every move, could mouth their words, make them seem like fools.

Though I was seeing into the past, my eye had wandered from the chicory by the driveway back to the Hawns' back door and their dining-room window, when all of a sudden their back door was flung open and Shirley came out carrying the baby Nellie whose mouth was opening into a cry. Shirley was herding the other two children ahead of her; they moved so fast I lost them and then found them again by the shed door where I saw Shirley butt the side door open with her hip, and then she and the children disappeared into the shed. Moments later, the garage door opened, and the brown Buick backed out fast and headed toward town. I aimed the telescope at the back door again and watched for Carl for a long time, but he didn't appear.

Carl. When I thought of him, I saw him that night in the driveway. I saw both of us as though I were a third person standing beside us. I saw his hands on my skin and heard the soft sound his hands made on my arms. I heard his breathing and my breathing. I remembered every part of the little that had happened, felt again where his knee pressed me, and saw his broad hands on my back. But these pictures did not stop with what happened. They went on without a seam to daydreams of my face raised and his mouth on mine and the pictures didn't stop there either.

When I put the telescope down, my feet and butt were numb from sitting there so long. It was about 9:30. If you were going to walk beans today, the rows would be dry by now; your jeans wouldn't get soaked with dew. I went in the house, went upstairs, ran the water for a bath. I hung up my nightgown on the back of the door, then walked from bedroom to bedroom while the water ran, and tried to decide if I really wanted to know what I was beginning to know about Carl and Shirley Hawn and did I really want to feel what I was feeling about Carl. What would I do with Carl Hawn and what would I do with this information about his marriage? What information? I knew almost nothing. Carl drank too much one night and stood too close to me. He wanted me to call Jack. Shirley and Carl fight now and then. What was that to know? Nothing really. People have fights all the time.

I stayed in the bathtub a long time. The window was open so the hot wind that I could imagine coming across miles of desert and plains blew across the bathwater. The parts of me not under the water dried off in the wind in seconds. I could hear a tractor somewhere, but I knew it wasn't Carl's. When I got out of the tub, I stood at one of the long bedroom windows facing the center of the farm until I was dry, then I put on my jeans and shirt. I found my purse and car keys, got in the car and headed for town. I'd go see Dad.

But two miles away, past the Hawns, I turned the car around fast at the edge of a field, knocking down a few rows of beans, and headed back to the Hawns.

I knew I shouldn't be doing this, so my mouth was dry and my knees were shaking when I got out of the car. I went in on the back porch and knocked at the door. The storm doors were still on. It was hot in there and smelled of cats and chicken feed. I knocked again as I rehearsed in my mind what I would say: Is Shirley here? I was just going in town and I thought I'd see if she needed anything. Or if you needed anything, Carl. No, I wouldn't say that last part. I knocked again, louder. There was no answer, no movement in the house. It was dark. The drapes were still drawn. The porch door behind me opened and there was Carl again standing with his back to the light.

"Hi, Carl. I just was on my way in town and I wanted to see if you want anything. From town. You or Shirley."

"The direction you came from, it looks like you're coming from town."

"Well, I got part way there, not very far, and thought I'd come ask."

"That's really, really thoughtful, Janet, really," Carl was smirking, "but we don't need a thing." Then Carl pushed past me as if I were one of the cats.

"I owe you some rent," I called after him as he disappeared into the house.

"Forget it, Jan," he called back as he went up the stairs.

"I'll talk to you later, Carl," but there was no answer, and I left with a sick feeling in my stomach, embarrassed and shaking.

I drove fast to the A & W drive-in on the outskirts of town, picked up Dad's favorites, and drove to the Half Moon Hotel. Dad was not on the porch with the old men. "He's in there watching his story," one of the men on the porch told me.

"His 'story'?"

"His soap. 'Love of Life'."

I went on into the stale, dim old lobby and down the hall to Dad's room at the south end of the first floor, next to the porch. "Come on in, Janet," I heard before I got halfway down the hall. His door was open. I figured it always was. I could not imagine my father alone in a room shutting anyone out.

"Hi, Dad, I brought you lunch. Two coney dogs and a root beer float."

"Great, perfect. Sit right down here," and he patted the sofa beside him. I moved aside a pile of clean laundry and sat down beside Dad who was watching a huge color television. "Where'd you get that, Papa?" Dad looked at me; I hadn't called him Papa in years.

"I sold a bunch of crap and bought myself it." He was still looking at me trying to figure out the "papa" business. I wasn't sure myself; I just felt young that day.

"It has a good picture," I said. "A big one, too."

"Yes, it does." He was still curious, but he began to unwrap a coney dog as I found the straw for the root beer float. "Where's yours?" he asked.

"Oh, I forgot. I'm not hungry."

Dad was beginning to watch his show again. A young man with long hair and love beads came into the office of a grey-haired man who evidently was a doctor. The grey-haired man was not glad to see this hippie. They were talking about someone named Heather. The hippie liked Heather; the older man did not. I had unwrapped the second hot dog and absent-mindedly eaten it.

Dad looked at the wrapper. "I guess I was hungry," I said.

"I guess so," Dad was only a little annoyed. We sat on the sofa together in the dim room and watched the people on TV knock on doors and ring doorbells, go into houses or offices, talk, drink something, leave. When the theme music came on and the credits rolled, Dad slapped my leg, stood up, walked over to turn off the TV and said, "Let's go get some more coney dogs."

But I wanted to go home. I hadn't talked for so long that I'd lost the hang of it. I felt far away from him and sad and I wanted to be by myself, so I said I had to go, but before I left town, in the Five and Ten I bought three pairs of yellow lace underpants.

On the way home, I turned down the little farm road that goes to the center of our section, and I parked the car on the rickety bridge over the drainage ditch. I got out of the car, waded through the tall grass and weeds that grew on the steep banks of the ditch, and sat down on the cool earth in the shade under the bridge. On the bush beside me, but in the sun, were ripe mulberries covered with ants as fat and black as blackberries. The grasses made a ragged edge against the sky. Doves on the wires sang their song like human sighing, and somewhere in the field a pheasant called its warning. For a few moments, as I sat there in the shade of the bridge and my eyes adjusted to the dark, it felt like I was sitting there in my own future, the deed done, the pleasure past, living in the ruins. I knew that walking around wanting Carl Hawn all the time made no sense except the sense that skin makes on skin. I shivered and moved out into the sun and lay back in the deep grass and closed my eyes. With my eyes shut, I felt how small I was on the surface of the earth, how small were the domes of my eyelids, how out of scale I was under all that blue. When I sat up and opened my eyes, I saw that, in the scheme of things, my wanting Carl Hawn was like this ant wanting to climb this stem. I lifted the ant off the stem and let it crawl on my arm. When it headed up my sleeve, I brushed it off. I don't have to have Carl, I told myself. I'll want something else. I'll want Jack. I'll replace these pictures in my mind with other pictures. Besides, who am I to act as if the domes of my eyes are the limits of the world? Who am I to act as if people for centuries haven't known that it's a bad idea to sleep with your neighbor's husband? I tried to think of Shirley, but I couldn't; I didn't care about Shirley. I tried to think of what the nuns had been telling me for years, but somehow, under that sky and in the middle of all the heat and fast green growth, what the nuns and priests had to say seemed irrelevant, silly, ideas suited for town life.

The trickle of the creek through the water weeds, the glint of the sun on the surface, the water striders, gradually made me forget what I was thinking about and I watched the mud at the bottom of the ditch until I could tell the difference between mud and greenish-brown crawdads and pieces of a rusty bucket, and then I could see suspended between the mud and the sun on the surface, hundreds of minnows like tiny weather vanes aiming upstream, aiming west, home. After a while, I got up and went home.

I continued to spend summer days sitting on the porch, looking through the spyglass because it seemed to me that anything a person could call useful or a quality with a capital letter was not something that would sit still with you in a room or on the porch. What was true seemed to me to be something I would be out of the picture of; it was something that existed when there was a frame and when the little figures in the frame were far away.

I could see very little of human drama through the telescope, but a great deal of landscape. When the light was right, I could once in a while see Shirley through their kitchen window. She sat at the kitchen table and smoked cigarettes. There was almost nothing I could make of the little I could see. One morning I aimed the spyglass haphazardly over there and I saw for a split second an apparition. What seemed to come into focus, I think, was a woman's bare breast. Just for a split second. But I lost it. I swung this one eye around there all morning, but there was no more movement, not a sign of life. Just that one beautiful, bare breast with sun on it went by my one eye. There was nothing that could be but a trick, a joke my mind or my eye was playing on me.

One afternoon, I could see over at Carl and Shirley's their little children playing in the driveway, grousing like sparrows in the gravel. Shirley was weeding in the garden. In the beanfield by the house, Carl walked up and back by himself. I watched his back and his shoulders as he hoed corn and pulled butterprint. I imagined the way parts of him might look, sounds he might make, words he might say. The children ran around and around the house. Mandy, the oldest, hid in the hydrangea to jump out at the little boy and scare him. Shirley carried a bushel basket of weeds to the trash heap behind the shed.

If there was drama, it was all off-stage in the house or in the squabbles of chickens, the picaresque strayings of dogs and cats. What was out there was the day-to-day that Carl breathed in and out, that filled his lungs and days, killed his time, grew his crops. I thought I was at a good distance from the Hawns and events, but I couldn't stop thinking about Carl.

One morning in late June I woke up worn out and disgusted with myself. I took a bath and washed my hair, made myself a good breakfast and ate it, wrote and typed some job-application letters and then I called my mom at work to ask her to meet me in town for supper.

"Sure, honey. What's wrong?" I could hear machines in the background and Muzak and a man laughing, a woman shouting. Mom lived in a world I couldn't even picture.

"Nothing. Just this job stuff. I don't know what to do."

"OK, honey, we'll talk later. I gotta get off this phone."

As I drove in town later on the back roads, the crickets in the fields on both sides of the road seethed like my breaths; my skin was dry and itchy and my hair irritated me. I couldn't stand it touching my face.

The first house in town was the last place I wanted to see. Ever since I was a girl, I had averted my eyes from Ruby and Pearl Giles' place. Ruby and Pearl were "old maids" who appeared to be ossified together in this falling-down house at the edge of town. At home, they stayed behind locked doors and closed windows obscured by unpruned shrubs. At weddings and funerals, their every word was a bitter spit or bite. No one liked them and they liked nothing.

Half Moon was full of women without men – widows of farmers, divorcees with three kids, old maids, so there were other versions in town of how to live unmarried. The town's correct and ideal version of a woman alone was that of Erie Beale, my – and everyone else's – first grade teacher. She was a woman who had always been fifty. She wore ladylike flowered dresses, wore her braided hair wrapped around her head in an old-fashioned way. She was generous and kind, so she not only had time to listen to your story, but she remembered it and could be trusted to, if she passed it along, tell your version of it in a quiet and ladylike voice. She apparently never thought of sex as something for herself. My sister Mary was a sadder version of a woman alone; she was quiet, Catholic, undemanding, bitter, chaste. My mother's version was almost the opposite of these. Mom was loud and independent and had lots of boyfriends. This version should have been compatible with mine, but because she was my mother, I guess, it just embarrassed me.

I passed Mary's house on the bumpy brick street, next door to the church where the lily of the valley grew outside the windows. For a few moments I missed the cold, damp, unchanging church air, missed knowing that I was in the right place at the right time, and I missed standing among all those people I knew. Dad, though he wasn't Catholic and thought Catholics were strange, used to take me to church when I was a girl living on the farm with him. He always took me to an early Mass and we were always late, so we'd stay for part of the next one, until Dad would poke me and say, "This is where we came in." One time when I was about ten I asked him why he bothered to take me to church. "Curiosity, kid, and besides I promised Edith." I remember several years later when I was a teen-ager complaining to my mother about what a sloppy farmer Dad was, she said, "Your father has only one characteristic, and most people have two or three. He has curiosity. He stands in need of pride or ambition or some mechanical ability. Any one of them would have saved our marriage."

As I passed St. Rose's, I half-heartedly resolved to start going to Mass again. Maybe that would make me stop thinking about Carl, but I knew I wouldn't really go.

Mom took me that evening to a new cafe in one of the storefronts on Main Street. It was new to me, but obviously Mom was a regular here; some of these people looked only vaguely familiar to me, but they all spoke to me by name, asked me how my job hunt was going, how had I liked college up north, and why didn't I move in town and live with my mother "where all the action is." I tried to be polite, but that place was too bright and hot and full of people with questions. Fried fish was brought to us without our having to order, and coleslaw and rolls. Mom smoked while she ate and carried on conversations with people four and five tables away.

The heat in there and the heavy smells of smoke and grease and the reverberating walls made going out into the night air even sweeter. As Mom and I walked the three blocks to her place where I had left my car, she began to tell me a long story about some guy at work who had slipped on blood on the floor and now he couldn't even lift his arm over his head, let alone a side of beef, but I couldn't listen. Flocks of starlings headed for the edge of town and the fields not far away. Neon seemed feeble against that red evening sky and so did the little sounds of human life that came through the screen doors. Only the fields were holding their own. I felt so small.

"Mom, I have these... longings sometimes."

"What for, honey?" Mom put her arm around me.

"For men." I stumbled on a brick, and as I reached out to keep myself from falling, I saw for a moment one of the boys from college whom I had walked away from, left when he was sound asleep. I saw Dan, naked, sleeping on his stomach, his mouth awry like a baby's, one arm hanging off the bed, fingers resting on the linoleum, curled under like the frayed ends of a rope. "I mean, for a man."

"My God, Janet, that's perfectly normal at your age. Hell, at my age, too." Though the streets were empty, I thought Mom was talking a little loud.

"I know, Mom, but it's so strong sometimes, it scares me. I mean it confuses me. I think of Carl Hawn... "

"You know he broke up with that girl that he was engaged to. Why don't you call him up? Girls can do that now. Or drive up to Madison, go see him." Mom had heard me say Jack Hawn. It was a close call. I was relieved and freed and sad. "I always thought that Jack was good for you, so I wouldn't worry about lusting after Jack. I'd worry if you *didn't* have the hots for somebody. Like I worry about your sister." I realized that Mom thought of lust only as the sticky stuff that catches men and seals them up.

After I left Mom's I turned west on Walnut Street to head out of town through the tunnel of soft maple trees. At the foot of the street were the fields, a wall of corn. It felt good to be driving out of town, west, home.

The next morning, from my bedroom window with my naked eye, I could see an orange truck backed up to Carl and Shirley's front door.

I went down and got the telescope and looked. It was a haul-it-yourself moving truck. Shirley and several of her brothers were loading what must have been Shirley's and the kids' things into the truck. Carl was standing in the side yard with his arms folded, watching. When the brothers got out a pink chest of drawers, Carl went to the shed and got his hoe, put it in the back of his pick-up, and drove out to the beanfield.

The brothers had put a big upholstered chair in the front yard to put in the truck, but they forgot it or there wasn't room. That chair was out there until August, until Jack came home.

CHAPTER 6

Carl

I woke early one morning around the first of July thinking of
Carl. I liked the bathwater feel of the air even at seven o'clock in
the morning. I liked to sweat, liked my clothes to stick to my
skin, liked to taste the sweat above my upper lip. The hotter the
better is the way I liked my weather.

Because the windows and curtains were open all night, the
cloth and metal surfaces in the house were as damp as grass.
Right away I thought of Carl in that empty house across the section. I ate my toast and drank my coffee in the yard. The morning air was cool under my loose nightgown. I knew I would
speak to no human being that day until I spoke to Carl Hawn.
All my weight was in my arms, my legs; they seemed to pull me
toward Carl with some horizontal gravity. I was a spider, all
limbs and mouth and metallic eyes, all grasp and suck, but I

wished Carl no harm. I just wanted to *have* him. I wished Jack no harm either.

After supper that evening I called Carl and asked him if I could come over. "Sure," he said.

The moon was almost full so I drove across the section with the car lights off; my left arm I stuck out the window to catch the night air and bugs.

Carl's house was dark, except for the blue light of the TV in the living room. Through the back-porch door I could see, in a square of moonlight on the kitchen floor, newspapers and a pot lid and a tennis shoe. While I was looking, one of their yellow cats walked through the square of light and disappeared.

If a house has no furniture, somehow you don't need to knock. I walked through the house to the living room where Carl, with a beer in his hand, was stretched out in a big chair with his feet propped on a styrofoam cooler. The little TV, which sat on a kitchen chair in front of him, sounded funny in the empty room. Carl looked up, took a drink of beer, waved me in. I went in and sat down on the arm of the chair he sat in. Carl moved his feet from the cooler and opened it, handed me a beer, and went back to watching the show. He was watching "Gunsmoke," which I usually liked, but this was the kind I hated – heartwarming, with nuns and orphans. Matt and Kitty and Chester were all stepping out of character to rescue these fools from bandits. Carl didn't seem to mind though.

When Matt and the nuns and orphans headed back across the prairie toward Dodge, Carl pulled me down to lie across his lap, and I watched the rest of the show with Carl's arms around me, my legs over the edge of the chair. I don't remember a thing. Those nuns and orphans may still be wandering in the desert. All I could do was try to believe that what I had daydreamed was really happening. I told myself over and over this is real, this is real. This is where I am. With Carl.

When the show was over, Carl said, "Let's go to town," and shoved me off his lap. When I stood up, he took my hand, "Come with me first. I want to put on a clean shirt," and he led me upstairs to his room. He turned on the top light and looked for a shirt while I wandered around the other empty rooms. From the sound of the wire hangers, I could tell Carl's closet was almost empty.

In the kids' rooms there were socks on the floor and pages out of books and broken dolls. The wheels of toy trucks. Candy wrappers. Just the sound of my footsteps told me how far Shirley had gone and what an awful thing had happened to Carl.

I came back and stood in the door while he buttoned his shirt. "Why'd she do this, Carl?"

"I don't know, really. Let's go to Bloomington, not Half Moon. You drive."

We went to a steak place, a huge dark place, fiercely air-conditioned and disinfected. Carl ate and drank, and I just shivered and fiddled with a salad and listened to him.

"Shirley says she wants to do man's work," he said. "She wants to work at Knacker Packing in Half Moon or she wants to drive a truck. I asked her why and she said, 'Man's work is more interesting and it pays. Besides, I want to get out of the house.' I said, 'Why do you want to get out of the house?' She said she's cooped up there. Then I said I would like to work in the house; it seems like nice work to me, but she just laughed." In a quieter voice, Carl said, "I used to think women and girls talked in a foreign language when men weren't there and I used to try to catch them at it. I don't know," and he sighed, "I think I would like to work in the house." Carl seemed to like it that I cried a little then, but I wasn't just crying for him; I was crying because I wanted him so much, I was afraid I would mess things up.

"Let's go," I started to say, when he put his hand on my arm and nodded toward two couples just walking in on the other side of the room.

Three of these people were big people, and the fourth one was my dad. Mr. Ed Check, all dressed up in a grey suit, pink shirt, white belt and shoes, and a wide, dark grey tie. There was a red carnation in his buttonhole. I ducked down, and Carl laughed. "Don't worry! He won't see us over here."

All four of these people wore flowers; the women wore corsages. This was evidently a big evening for these people. Then I realized that my dad was *with* one of these women, and from the looks of things – his hand rested lightly on her hip as they crossed the restaurant – they were having a good time. This big-boned woman with frizzy hair looked to be about thirty-five. She was wearing a black and silver dress that looked like Christmas wrapping paper, cut to drape gracefully over the hips, but her hips filled up the drape. Her face was pretty, though, and she looked strong, like she was more comfortable in blue jeans than a dress.

"She looks like a truck-stop waitress on the Indiana Turnpike," I said. "Why is Dad out with a woman like her?"

Carl laughed at me. "Now, don't be mean. For the same reasons I'm out with a woman like you. The same reasons you're out with a man like me." Carl was still laughing.

"But he looks like an. . . "

"Asshole?"

Carl leaned toward me, tipping over his almost-empty beer glass. "Listen, Janet, Ed's my friend. He's no asshole. That's Marlene Whiteside and I hear she is divorced, but is real nice and teaches speed reading at the high school." Carl looked beyond me at Dad, who I could see was pulling a chair out for the lady, bowing a little. "But he does look like an asshole, doesn't he?" We both laughed, then, and got out of there.

As we were walking to the car, Carl put his arm around my waist. "Did you ever call Jack?" He was trying to make this a joke.

"No."

"Why not?"

"I don't know."

"I know."

Before we got to the car, he put his arms around me and held me to the length of him. "Let's have some time together," he said in my ear. I felt his breath and lips move my hair. "Some *times.*"

We started kissing then, and I don't know how we got home like that. We spent the next twenty-four hours together, in my house. We must have slept some and eaten a little, but I don't remember. I learned a lot, how to wait and how to take things easy.

For the next few weeks I was either with Carl or waiting for Carl – always in my house, never in his. We didn't talk much; this was not a social thing. Carl was like weather to me, inside and out, and there is no point talking to the weather. Sometimes he did try to tell me things, usually about his children, but I always thought of a good reason for him not to talk. No one else called or came out. I was cut off from everyone but Carl, descending into paradise, into summer; I was under the weather.

One time I put on a yellow dress and took some iced tea to him out in the field. When he stopped the tractor by the ditch, I led him to a place where Joyce and I used to play.

This was a little piece of prairie, never plowed or mowed because the glacier left five boulders there. We trampled down some of the six-foot grass in the hollow between the rocks, "like giant rabbits," Carl said. When we sat down we were in a quiet room and the hot wind went by above us. We pulled a little grass back over us for shade.

"Why didn't you ever bring me here when we were kids?"

"This was for girls then."

"Now it's liberated?"

"Right."

The sound of the wind whipping the grass and corn around seemed far away. We drank tea out of the jar and took all our clothes off, and when our breathing quieted down later, we could hear the trickle of water in the ditch. Even then I was telling myself, remember this when you're eighty; remember your yellow dress, his blue shirt, the feel and smell of the crushed grass. Remember the warm smell of sun on weeds, the dry wind in the grass above us, the cricket chirping. And most of all, remember how your neighbor's strong back felt under your hands, remember the taste of the sweat of your neighbor's brow, the feel of his mouth on the palm of your hand like a small animal.

No one came out from town, and no one called. The grass grew tall in our yards. We never shut any windows or any curtains, never locked any doors. A lot of work didn't get done, but the corn was growing and the beans were beginning to ripen.

On the Fourth of July, we sat on my front porch and watched fireworks in three towns. It felt like we were watching a war in another country or a festival on another planet.

One evening I was sitting on the step when Carl drove up and got out of the truck with an odd look on his face. He was holding his hands funny in front of his chest. He stood in front of me and told me to unbutton his shirt. When I did, two little yellow kittens stuck their heads out. "These are for you," he said. When I took the scared little cats out of his shirt, I saw there were tiny scratches all over his chest.

There was no rain. I took long baths. The little cats sat on the edge of the tub and batted at the water. Sometimes I could hear Carl's tractor. He was cultivating in the field next to the house. Up and back. Up and back. The wind was hot and every day the rain we thought maybe-this-afternoon didn't come. Field dust settled on the floors, and there were footprints of two humans and two cats in the dust. I could hear Carl on the tractor in the field. Going up and down the field, slow, wrapped in the dust. The man and machine floating across the surface.

Sometimes he'd stop work in the middle of the day and we'd go upstairs and take a bath. Field dirt left a muddy delta in the tub.

Dust hung over the fields; it was so dry. Every day he'd say, "Maybe today some rain." Sometimes it rained half a mile away, but not a drop here. We could smell it, though, and see it like grey sheets over other farms. "It's raining somewhere," he'd say, "someone's getting some rain." On afternoons like that, all my wanting was a hard little ball under my breastbone. I was a baby, next to Carl's want-want-want for our neighbor's rain clouds.

I paced the house when he was gone. The little cats attacked my heels and ankles. I woke from naps in the afternoon with the dusty smell of cats in my nose. When we were in bed, more than once a cat or two jumped on Carl's back and he flung it across the room.

We were almost silent in those weeks, though now and then in the dark Carl would talk. One night he told me that once, ten years or so ago, he stood next to the railroad tracks with some other farmers in town. He didn't remember what they were doing there that night, but there were three others besides him, and they'd been talking under the light on the side of the grain elevator office when a long freight went through. They had felt it with their feet when it was still a long way off, and then, down that track that doesn't curve for forty-some miles, they saw the white light coming worming its way. When the freight was on them, deafening, barreling through, they all, oddly, stepped a little closer to it. He said they sort of lined up parallel to the tracks with their hands in their pockets, and raised their faces to it, to the battering turbulence it made in the night air.

Illinois was thick with humidity or dust or heat or all of those, and time and Carl and I seemed to move slowly in it. I was way below the surface in this, wordless, and there was always a pleasant, but drowning, sensation. Now and then, through this air, this time, I could see all that I was shutting out, but I couldn't hear any voices. Light carried through this air, but no sound.

One of the mornings that Carl was working nearby in the field, I walked on the little road out to the center of our square-mile section. High clouds were moving fast from west to east and the sky above them was the summer's blue. I realized that we live between land and sky, on the frontier between two great countries. I had forgotten how sky is as much a country to live in as land. I had forgotten that we live in the sky and under it; we live on the land. From the west were rolling pile after pile of fat, white, complicated clouds, and above the clouds was the clear and uncomplicated blue. I thought of blue, white, and gold roccoco ceilings, and I had to look down, away from all that motion and grandeur. This sky was hard to live up to. It brought me messages from other times and places and made me lonely. I was as confused on that flat land under all that sky as any stranger would be, and my limbs ached from all this local wanting and getting. Image after image of the clouds as cities, as ceilings, ghosts, pasts, and saints rolled over me, as did the clouds themselves. I had to sit down on the dirt and watch the ants at their mining.

When I stood up again, I saw clearly that the land, the farm where I was standing, was the bottom of a vast lake. The clouds sailed on an invisible surface in swifter currents high above. Small eddies, messages, reached my ears from the wash of that great migration and rumors reached me from the frontier. "These are the gifts for those who move on. These are the names of far places."

Carl and I were living on what happens on the surface of the skin.

It finally did rain one afternoon in the middle of August. We sat on my porch and watched the low, black, straight-edged border of the rain overtake us. At first the light was violently green and the wind was cold, and there was lightning and thunder all around us. Then the rain came, blustery at first, then straight down; it settled in to rain the rest of the day. In the kitchen we were closed in by the rain and I felt safe. Carl leaned over, looking out the window above the sink. I stood at the screen door smelling the rain and listening to it.

With my face pressed to the screen, I smelled the wet rust and dust and wood. Rain had blown up onto the porch. I noticed the green paint was peeling from the door frame, there were holes in the rusty screen, the door sill was damp and rotten. At that moment, I didn't care, but I thought one of these days I *will* care and I'll try to fix things up. At that moment, I liked everything just the way it was. I liked the grey, soaked sky and all that shiny green. I liked the drone of the rain on the roof, the spattering from the gutters onto the porch steps, the drip of single drops on the leaves of the vines. I liked the smell and the cool of the rain. When I lifted my forehead off the screen, I saw that there were raindrops trapped all over the screen like hundreds of square lenses and that in each of those lenses I could see a perfect, tiny version of the green and grey world I was so satisfied with. I could hear Carl moving around in the kitchen behind me, beginning to fix supper. Then he turned the light on and I turned to help him.

That night in bed in the dark, after several breaths drawn as preamble, he told me he'd asked Shirley "again" to come back, to bring the kids home. "I wanted you to know that," he said, "to be fair."

After a while I asked him what she said.

"She said she won't come back, but she'll talk to me in town."

"What did you say?"

"I said I'd talk to her in town."

"Did you tell her about . . . this?"

"Of course not. I'm not a *damn* fool."

After that night Carl didn't come over any more. I waited and, through the telescope, watched him drive off every morning to talk to Shirley.

I was scared of what I felt. I was surprised at the strength of my feeling when I thought of him with another woman. The pain in my chest and the stomach aches and crying were somehow the reverse of all that wanting Carl and all that getting him. I was turned inside out. I felt like he had pulled the bones out of me, just when I was liking so much the way my own muscles and skin fit on them. I cried, I swore, I kicked things, I ate too much. What I didn't want to do, yet, was talk to anyone. I just wanted Carl back and I wanted not to hurt and feel this rage.

But all the time I was having these fits, I was watching myself. I was disgusted with this display even though no one saw it but me and the cats. I caught myself faking it now and then. I was hurt, but somehow I knew I wouldn't be hurt for long. I was crying my eyes out, but at the same time keeping an eye peeled for a good reason to get on with things.

One day near the house, at the edge of the beanfield, I pulled up a little stalk of volunteer corn. That squeak when the stalk slipped out of the lower leaves was in my body's memory. And so was the wet stalk, the clean smell of it, its relationship to thirst, the heft and balance of the stalk in my hand. It needed to be thrown. My hand and arm still remembered, and so did my back, the easy way to aim and throw the corn's perfect arc, remembered the festive rattle of the leaves in flight, and remembered the solid thud when it hit a neighbor boy square in the back. I felt a little better. I ran into the shed and, sure enough, there stuck behind a two-by-four beside the work bench, were three machetes, corn knives. I took the sharpest and went back out to the field. I would work for my neighbor, I would walk beans. I started there near the shed, cleaned out a whole patch of corn and weeds, and, for Carl, each of the stalks of corn I sailed through one of the little panes in the shed windows. When the corn was gone and the windows were all broken, I counted the panes: thirty-six. Then I went in the shed and counted the stalks of corn lying on the floor: forty-seven. Not bad for girls' rules. Not bad for a girl.

The next morning I got up late. I was listless and irritable and sick of my own company. I got dressed and went in town to see Dad.

When I got to the hotel, Dad was on his way out to the A & W for lunch. So I got in his car which was littered with crumbs and paper and went with him. We parked at the A & W facing the second-growth hedge that separated it from the laundromat. The air smelled of french fries and fabric softener and fresh-cut grass. Dad pushed the button on the call box and summoned the voice of an amplified teen-ager who answered so loud we had to put our fingers in our ears. "Good afternoon, can I take your order?" made us both almost scream, but Dad was ready for it, "Four coney dogs, root beer float, and black coffee to eat here. And nothing else."

Dad turned to me. "Listen to this. You'll love this."

The voice — half machine, half teen-ager — squawked again. "Would you like some fries with your order?"

"She always says that!" Dad was laughing and wiping tears from his eyes. "No fries!" he hollered back.

"Cream in your coffee?" she asked.

"Black, I said, goddamn it!"

"Will that be for here or to take out?"

"For here!" The silly, awful voice was driving us mad.

It was funny and I was on the verge of appreciating it, but I couldn't yet. I felt like I was floating to the surface, to the real air where other people breathed and laughed, but I wasn't quite there yet.

"Dad, why don't you just go in? Why do you put up with that?"

"Janet, what the hell's wrong with you? Where's your sense of humor?"

"Nowhere."

"No shit!"

While we waited for our food, Dad noticed and named the wild plants in the hedge — sumac, box elder, wild cherry, chicory, black-eyed Susan. He said, "Did you know chicory isn't a native plant? I didn't either. I read it someplace the other day. It comes from China, I think, or Europe. I forget now. Let's take our lunch to the park."

Half Moon has two parks — one up on one of the hills at the center of town and the other at the foot of the hills beside the river. Both parks had the names of good citizens, but everyone called them High Park and Low Park. There was no car in the parking lot but ours. We parked behind one of those telephone pole barriers; ahead of us was a stretch of worn-out grass and beyond that was a strip of packed-down brown dirt and then an opaque backwater of the Sugar River. I didn't want to bother getting out, so we rolled the windows all the way down and ate in the car.

Eating outdoors in this park would not be getting closer to nature. Ratty-looking ducks shat and shed all over the grass. The stagnant water was covered with duck fluff and pollen and algae. Leathery red cannas looked as fake and cheap as flamingos.

I was silent and sullen, but I was feeling better.

While we ate, Dad looked thoughtful. Then, when we finished eating, Dad asked, as if he'd come to a conclusion, "What's going on out at the farm?"

It took me awhile to get ready to answer. Before I did, Dad, who was watching a mother duck and some young ones swim up the river, said, "Not much, huh?"

"Not much." I saw as I said that a picture of Carl's little girl's pink bureau being carried through their front yard.

"You walking beans for Carl?"

"No, Dad, and I've hardly talked to anybody since the day of the sale." I thought for a moment, then I asked him, "What's this about a woman named Marlene something? Do you see her very often? Is it a big deal?"

"I thought you hadn't been talking to anybody." Dad put his arm out the window and adjusted his side mirror up and down, up and down. "I see her and I like her and that's all I can say. I have a right to see her and I suppose you have a right to ask, but I don't have anything to say about her." After a moment he looked at me and said, "You would like her, I think. Everybody does."

I couldn't think about her and I couldn't really think about him. "Did you know that Shirley took the kids and left?"

"Yeah, but she'll be back, Janet."

"How do you know?"

"That's what the word is around town. Carl and Shirley are negotiating now."

"What's it about?"

"I don't know and I don't want to know."

The ducks were out of sight now. Dad turned to me. "Did Carl ever ask you for any rent?"

"No, he said to forget it."

"Well, don't you forget it. I don't want you staying out there for nothing. I want you to pay rent or get out of there. I don't know why you want to be there anyway, under those circumstances. The place is falling down, depressing."

"I like it there."

"I know, so do I. But it's different now. I want you to go over there and give Carl two hundred dollars. If you haven't got it, I do." Dad pulled a wad of bills out of his breast pocket. He counted off ten twenties and handed them to me. "Take these to Carl. And begin to think of something to do, some place else to live, before your mother arranges the whole rest of your life for you, though I happen to agree with her on this one."

"What are you talking about? What is she up to?"

Dad laughed and shook his head. "Jack Hawn's coming home next week or so, and I think it's partly her doing. I'll be glad to see him, too, I have to say. I'll be glad when he's back for good. I like the way things are with Jack around."

I could barely breathe. For a moment I thought I was going to faint. My head had burst through into real light and real air. "How *are* things with Jack around?"

"I don't know, but I would say that with Jack Hawn things seem simpler and you can see the possibilities."

CHAPTER 7

Jack Comes Home

The rest of the summer happened in a different light, in thinner and clearer air. And the rest of the summer happened fast. Though a lot of things happened between the two events, sometimes it seems that I was standing at the sink eating a peach and, the next thing I knew, I was married to Jack.

First, I was eating that peach. I was standing at the sink, leaning over it so the juice would drip there and not on the floor, when three things occurred to me all in a row: 1. Carl leaned here like this that night we watched the rain; 2. If Jack saw me now – still in my nightgown at ten o'clock, hair sticking up funny, peach juice running down my arm – he would look away in real embarrassment and disgust; and 3. Grandma Check would call me trash. I was standing in Carl's shoes, feeling the ghost of Grandma Check come at me from behind, and listening for Jack to turn in the driveway. All summer I had rattled around in that house and then there I was crowded by a ghost, a former lover, and Jack. At that moment, the ghost was the most real to me. I could almost feel her heavy footfalls coming down the stairs and her eyes on my back as she bore down on me from the dining room. I was a kid again and I could hear her say to me as if I were going to — at nine years old — leave and set up housekeeping that week: "Jan, no matter how bad things get, never let your people stand at the zink," as she called it, "and eat out of pots. Trash do that." Trash. I hadn't yet washed my face. Peach juice had made muddy spots on one of my bare feet. I looked around me. The two cats were eating dried macaroni-and-cheese out of a plate on the floor. Near the refrigerator, there was some old cat shit. Long dead neighbor ladies were looking over my shoulder at the crusted dishes in my sink. Grandma's voice was in my head. Trash.

I began to clean the house that day and I cleaned for four days straight. All the junk, except the blue table and chair I had found around the farm and dragged in, I put in a heap and burned. The raggedy curtains I burned. The cats were banished to the outdoors; they were farm cats after all. The splintery wood floors and worn linoleum were scoured. Every corner was cleaned of cobwebs and house dust and field dirt. I kept wondering — am I getting ready to leave or to settle in? It alternately felt like both. I felt strobe lit. I didn't know if I was coming or going.

After I cleaned, I drove to town for some groceries and for canning supplies. I thought even then that canning is a fairly obvious purification ritual, but I was pretty sure it would make me feel better, help me deserve something, and I was right. One of my greatest pleasures that summer was coming home to that clean-smelling kitchen that day and putting away the groceries and setting things up for making spiced crab apples. I filled my new blue graniteware canning pot with water and turned on the heat under it. I sterilized a dozen quart jars and kept them hot in the oven. I covered the kitchen table with clean white dish towels, and put the rims and lids in a dish of hot water on the table. I laid out a ladle and funnel, and clean cloth to wipe the rims, and red-and-white labels for the jars. I measured out sugar and cinnamon and cloves and set them out on the counter. I knew what to do and how to do it because I had watched and helped Grandma and Mom put up spiced apples many times, but until that day I hadn't noticed what I knew or else I hadn't counted the knowledge for anything. Now all I needed was the crab apples.

I took a clean, white bed sheet and went out to the side yard to what we had always called the orchard, though all that was left of the original orchard was the crab apple that I was headed for, an old, split apple tree, and a peach tree where the little, hard, green peaches had never ripened before they fell off. I spread the sheet under the crab apple on the rippling, tall grass, and weighted it at the four corners with rocks from the driveway. Then I climbed up in the tree and began to drop down the crab apples onto the sheet. They were fairly big this year, a little bigger than a baby's fist, red and yellow like marzipan apples. They landed softly on the sheet in the grass.

When I had enough apples, I stayed up in the tree for a while, feeling how odd for a person was the motion of a tree in a wind, with the branches for bones and the breeze for nerves and muscle. Hearing the wind in the leaves from inside the tree made me feel long-haired and blind. I closed my eyes and felt too the slim branch that stretched me, that the length of me rested on. When I climbed down, I gathered up the corners of the sheet and carried the crab apples in slung on my back. In the kitchen, I filled the now-clean sink with cold water and washed the apples. The cheerful, neighborly bump of the crab apples on the sides of the sink scared off the ghosts of the past and the future, and settled me in to the here and now.

I worked slowly and methodically and happily in the kitchen that smelled like cinnamon and cloves, but a dozen quarts of spiced apples were lined up on the counter too soon. There were more jars and more crab apples so I started some crab apple jelly. When the clear juice was dripping into a pan through a dish towel, I called Carl and Shirley's and Carl answered the phone.

"Is Shirley back yet, Carl?" I asked without preliminaries.

"No," he said, "Why?" Carl sounded wary of me.

"What's happening to the stuff out in your garden?"

"Nothing. It's just out there."

"Well, I'm going to come get it and can it. There's no sense in it spoiling."

Carl didn't say anything.

"I won't come in. I'm just going to run over now and pick what's there and when I'm done canning I'll give you guys half."

"If you want." Carl was still wary.

I drove over and spent more than an hour picking. I didn't have baskets, so I was putting tomatoes, peppers, green beans, and peas in pillowcases and dish towels. It was hot out there, and my arms were covered with the green from tomato plants and prickers from cucumbers.

After awhile, Carl came out of the house and helped me. He looked thin. We just talked about the vegetables: "Take these, too," and "Do you want any of these?"

When we were carrying the stuff to my car, I said, "Carl, Dad gave me money to give you for rent, but I've spent some of it on groceries and canning supplies and I'm going to need more jars."

"I don't want any rent from you or your dad. He should know that."

"He doesn't want me to sponge off you." As soon as I said it, I saw it literally, me on top of Carl, trying to absorb Carl.

Carl must have seen it that way too because for a minute he

looked like he might run, but he stood his ground, and then he said, "Shirley and the kids are moving back next week."

I said, "Carl, I'm so glad." And I was. But I didn't dare look at him. I felt other things too besides gladness, so I didn't look at him. I wanted to stay this new way I was, this simple way.

"And, Janet," he said as he lifted a pillowcase of tomatoes into the trunk of the Mustang, "Jack will be here day after tomorrow."

"Fine," I said, again without looking at him. Then I heard myself say, though I almost didn't have enough breath for the whole sentence, "You and him come over for supper that night, and I'll call Dad and the others to come too."

"You sure you want to do that?"

"Why not?" I said, and, this time looking at him, I said again, "Why not?" thereby finishing things up somehow, sealing them away.

After a minute, Carl said, "Then I better mow over there or nobody will be able to find the place." His voice was light and easy; he was glad to be rid of me.

I went home and canned tomatoes until midnight. I let the cats back in the house to have someone to talk to and we listened to the radio. The cats sat on top of the refrigerator like those chartreuse ceramic panthers used to sit on television sets, and they watched my every move. The beautiful red jars lined up on the white dish towels made me rich, but virtuous. I knew I could take these riches through the eye of any needle.

I canned all the next day and had to go to town for more jars. In town, I stopped at Dad's; he said he'd be pleased to come out for dinner the next day. I called Mom at work, but she wouldn't come because Dad was going to be there and, besides, didn't I know he was going out with "some young chick." I stopped at my sister's and asked her to come out too. She said she didn't think she would, but why don't I come to her place instead. "Not this time," I said, then I borrowed from her some pretty blue plates and cloth napkins and some glasses and silverware.

The morning that Jack and Carl and Dad were to come to dinner, I got up early to the sound of Carl mowing the side yards with the tractor mower. Later, with the smaller riding mower, he mowed in front. While he was out there, I went out and waved him to come in. He was a little reluctant, but he stopped the mower and followed me into the house where I opened my kitchen cupboard and showed him, ta-da, my beautiful rows of jars of canned apples, pears, tomatoes, peas, jelly, applesauce, beans, and more.

"Half of these, at least, are yours," I said. "For you and Shirley and the kids. In a day or so, when I've looked at them enough, I'll bring them over."

"They are pretty," Carl said with his hands in his pockets, "like crops." He turned and got a drink at the sink and went back out to his mowing.

He and Dad and Jack would be here at about five. It was only eleven, but I was almost ready. I'd made chicken and noodles first thing that morning. I was amazed at how much I remembered about making farm-lady noodles, and it's a good thing, too, because I didn't have any cookbooks. But I could still see Mom and Grandma piling the flour on a board and putting the egg in the little crater; I could still see the kneading and feel when the dough was right, and now my noodles were cut and drying draped over a broomstick across two chairs just like they were supposed to be. The chicken was poached and boned and the sauce was made. Tomatoes for the salad were picked and washed and beside a nice blue plate ready to be sliced. Beans were snapped and in the pot with some onion. I just had to add a little water and cook them. I had made a chocolate cake. It looked nothing like the one on the cocoa can but I would serve it sliced and they would never know the top layer slid off. I didn't know what wine was correct with chicken and noodles, so I had bought beer.

I knew everything about what we would eat, and when, and who would be there, but I hadn't figured out where we would eat.

I thought we should eat outside; the day was clear and not real hot, and since the summer had been so dry, we didn't have many mosquitoes. I wandered around outside where Carl had mowed with the tractor mower and found the perfect spot – between the L-shaped osage orange hedge and the house, in the square side yard where the lawn, somewhat shaded by the hedge, was greener than the rest of the sun-burnt grass. Carl hadn't taken the riding mower back yet, so I started it and mowed in the six-inch deep, hacked-off grass a nice, neat dining-room-sized square in the center of the yard. Then I hauled the blue table out there and then washed a red Indian-print bedspread and put it on the table damp so it would dry without wrinkles by suppertime. I hauled out four chairs and four blue plates and the knives and forks and glasses. Blue napkins and yellow candles. And flowers, black-eyed Susans in a canning jar. It really looked pretty, so pretty I sat under the hedge at the edge of the yard for a while just looking at the red and blue and yellow table against the green grass.

The day seemed to go so slowly. I finished up the cooking and took a bath and washed my hair and put on my yellow dress. I looked all right too. I looked at myself in the bathroom mirror: I was thin and tan and my hair, though I needed a haircut, was shiny. Then I went downstairs and got the telescope and took it up to my bedroom and I aimed it at the Hawns' back yard.

Even before I focused and before I saw more than a blurred forearm go past my eye, I knew that was Jack's arm. And then there was Jack. The back of Jack. He was standing in front of Carl who was sitting on the steps drinking a beer. From the back, I could tell that Jack was working his persuasion on Carl. His gestures with his long arms were wide; they used almost the whole circle that his arms were the diameter of. His shoulders moved independent of each other. The back of his head was somehow eloquent, looking out for itself, commenting to you on Jack's speech, undermining it. I had never seen until then how much Jack was like Nelda, his mother. I could squint and fade out Jack and fill in Nelda who used space in the same way, though much less of it; Jack was big for a man, and Nelda was small for a woman.

In the old days, when she was the woman of that house, before she and D.E. retired to travel in their recreational vehicle, you could walk in that kitchen any time and she would be there padding around in her bare feet, and she would come up to you, even if she'd seen you two hours before, and standing square in front of you, put out her two arms and squeeze your two elbows to you and look you right in the eye and ask you, "When are you going to stop wearing so much eye shadow?" or "How's your grandma? Did she get out of bed yet?" It was hard to lie to her. You could do it, but you had to be ready ahead of time. And you had to plan ahead to avoid Nelda's plans, because she had figured out everyone's problem and the solution to it: The way to keep my mom and dad together was to get my aunt to deed the land to Dad and get Mom to quit that job at Knacker; and the way to get Grandma out of the bed she stayed in for twenty years was to stop waiting on her. Nelda was long on answers, but short on details. All the answers were somehow in that circle that her arms made all around her; answers seemed juggled, all in the air at once, dazzling, conjured faster than other human eyes could see. After Nelda looked you in the eye and held you there and told you what she wanted you to hear, she would let go of you, but you were not free; what was free were her arms to work out the answers, to carve out the air and use up some of yours.

Though Jack and Carl were outdoors in the yard, I could tell from the expression of Carl's body that Jack was using up some of Carl's air. Carl looked down, away from Jack's face, looked at his own legs stretched out in front of him and sometimes he examined the beer can he held as if he could see through it into the way things seemed before Jack showed up. But I knew from experience that it's hard to remember your own reasons when Jack is telling you his. I could see that Jack was bringing new things into Carl's reluctant consideration. The circle of Jack's arms was describing the wide world on the horizon, and on Carl and me, that wide world began to close in — bright-colored and varied, complex and old and terrible. We both were forced to take more into consideration. Carl's resistance, which was at first distance and irony, was slipping and shifting into something else, and partly it was fear.

Then Carl crumpled the beer can he held and threw it under the bushes by the porch, where I saw two cats investigate and delicately lick it. When I moved my eye back to Jack and Carl, I saw that Carl had given in. Jack was standing in front of him with his hands on his hips, and now Carl was moving his shoulders as if to relax them or loosen them or adjust some load, and now he was smiling up at Jack. Jack sat down next to Carl on the step and put an arm around Carl's shoulder and squeezed him until it occurred to Carl that he could get up and go in the house and get them some more beer. He brought the beers and sat down a little way from Jack on the step and then I could see their two faces side by side.

Carl's face was a Hawn's face — wide, blank planes; squinted, slanted eyes; irritable and secretive and inward-looking. Jack's face was just an American face. There was nothing in it that was peculiar or regional or Hawnish. It seemed to hold no secrets. You could open any magazine and see Jack Hawn in the ads; you could turn on the TV and there Jack's face would be. What was different about Jack was his energy, I guess, his drive and what he dreamed. But even that wasn't all that special. Jack's dream was to own some land and a house and some farm equipment and to farm, in the most modern and scientific way, all the rest of his life. He wanted a wife and children and he was willing to be modern about that too. This was after all the sixties, and Jack, though he was at heart a conservative man, was more aware of the times than any of the rest of us. Jack had a conscience; the rest of us just had skin.

When I put the telescope down, I wished Carl had put up more of a fight. But how could I think that? I didn't even know what it was about. I made myself busy. I decided to put out some spiced apples and some applesauce, so I had to figure out what dishes to serve them in. I put the flowers in a blue jar instead of the clear one. And I decided at the last minute to iron the blue napkins that I had just smoothed out and folded nicely. I had no ironing board, so when Jack and Carl walked in the back door and through the kitchen, I was kneeling in the sun on the empty dining-room floor ironing a blue-flowered napkin on a green towel. I can still see the tiny blue flowers with red centers and the frayed edge of the olive-green towel when I think of their footsteps coming through the house.

"Get off your knees, Woman; you don't have to kneel to me. Maybe to King Carl here, but not to a peasant like me."

That was Jack, and he came right over and hauled me to my feet by my elbow and gave me a big, rough, public hug. Then he handed me a six-pack and said, "Don't say I never brought you anything."

Carl, standing in the doorway, said, "Give me that. I'll put it in the refrigerator and get the rest of the beer out of the car." He took the beers out of my hand and went out.

Jack stood in front of me holding my arms at my sides and looked at my face and I looked at his. He was almost the same, though maybe a little heavier — very nice to look at, his face open and determined. But there was a new transparency around his eyes, a faint darkness that circled them, so that his face, besides telling you things, seemed to ask you unanswerable questions, seemed to ask for you, and seemed to accept whatever you had to offer. Though I didn't know it then, those eyes of his would become over the years his most dominant feature, and the need and the loss of hope displayed there would be what, I think, cost him so many jobs in so many interviews. No one would hire a man who needed one so much. But then, at the beginning, it was all contradicted by his voice and his strong arms.

"How are you, Janet? You look skinny. I don't want you to get too skinny." His grip on my arms loosened and his hands were gentle on my arms like cloth, and then, with both hands, he pushed my hair away from my eyes. "And you could use a haircut." He let my raggedy hair fall through his fingers. "I'll give you a haircut." And then he turned and hollered, "Carl!" He was then walking out the back door and I was following him.

"Carl," he said when we were outside. "We're going to give this girl a haircut."

Carl was sitting in Jack's car, a Cutlass, with the door open, his feet in the driveway, holding a can of beer between his thighs. He had to lean out of the way when Jack opened the glove compartment and took out some barber scissors in a plastic case.

I was protesting. Jack didn't know how to cut hair. But already I was having the time of my life.

"We're going to cut Jan's hair," Jack said again.

"We aren't either," Carl said. "We don't know how to cut hair." Carl was laughing too and not really protesting.

"I cut my own all the time." Jack's dishwater blond hair was nondescript. Nobody could call him a hippie, but nobody could call him a redneck either.

"Where'll she sit?" Carl asked.

"You don't need to sit down to get your hair cut. That's just an old wives' tale. Carl, go in and get me a couple of dish towels out of the kitchen while I plan my strategy."

We were standing on the cement slab outside the back door and Jack was holding me and turning me around and around like I was a pot he was making. While Carl was in the house, one of those turns brought his hand gently across my breasts.

"You've changed, Jack," I said. "You didn't used to be so fast," and I pushed his hand down.

"I'm in a hurry, now," he said, looking at my hair and feeling it between his fingers. "We've got to get on with it, Janet. We've been wasting time."

"With the haircut?" I asked, though I knew what he meant.

Then Carl was there with the two dish towels which Jack draped over my shoulders. "Yeah, the haircut," Jack said. "We've got to get on with this haircut." Then, in his big, public voice he said, "It's just like pruning shrubs. All there is to it is getting both sides even. Carl, you stand behind me and make sure it's even."

We all held our breaths while Jack cut and I closed my eyes until Carl burst out laughing. "What?!" I said, wiping the hair off my face.

"Nothing, Janet, really nothing. Jack's giving you a fine hair cut," but he kept giggling, which made Jack turn around and stare at him and nick me a little in the neck. I tried to get away, but Jack would not allow that. Then there was a lot of giggling and scuffling around, like in the old days, and then Dad drove up and got out of the car, walking slowly and smiling and shaking his head. I saw him stand there watching us, grinning from ear to ear, like this is just what he's always wanted to see. After a few moments, he came over and pushed Jack aside and said, "Stand back, young man. You never asked me if you could cut my daughter's hair."

"I'm asking you now, sir," said Jack, and he knelt down flamboyantly in the grass, flourishing the scissors. "I'm asking you, sir, for the hair of your daughter in . . . " And then Jack collapsed on the grass in laughter, really hysterical laughter. The rest of us just looked at each other. Then Jack came to his knees again, still laughing. "I can't believe I'm going to say this like this. I had it all planned so different."

Then Jack jumped up and ran to the trunk of the Cutlass, opened it and took out a big cooler which he brought over and set down in front of us and opened. In it were four bottles of champagne. "See," he said, "I was ready to do it by the book." He was kneeling in front of the cooler and we were all quiet now while he was fishing around in his pocket. My heart was beating so hard I could barely hear, but I did hear.

"Do what by the book?" Dad asked. I looked at all three of them. They were all looking at me. Carl knew what Jack was going to say. He smiled at me while Jack put a small jeweler's box in my hand.

Jack was squeezing my hand around that box. "Do what?" Jack repeated. "Why ask for the hair of your daughter in matrimony, of course."

We all whooped in laughter, then hugged and held each other. I could barely breathe, the pressure of those arms was so great; we were like a star collapsing on itself. I tried to wipe my eyes on the sleeve of Jack's shirt while he was being pounded on

the back by my dad and then by Carl. And then Dad was jump-
ing up and down like a leprechaun yelling, "Hooray! Yippee!
Hooray! Yippee! You two sure took your time about all this!"

Then Jack took the towel off my shoulder and started to open
one of the bottles of champagne, when Carl's hand reached out
and stopped him. "Wait a minute Jack. Aren't you going to give
her a chance to say yes or no?"

"Oh, yeah, good idea!" Jack put the champagne down, and
held me at arms' length with those hands he'd just taken out of
the cooler. "Well?" he said.

I waited. Of course I would say yes, what else could I say, but
I waited, for effect.

"Well?" he said louder, squeezing my arms.

"Well, OK," I said. "Why not?"

And that's how Jack proposed to me and that's how I accepted
his proposal.

I guess the supper was good. I don't remember about the food.
I remember that my hair felt strangely lopsided, and I remember
that during supper, when I ran in the house to get the napkins, I
discovered we'd almost burnt the house down because the iron
was still on in the dining room.

We all drank too much out there in the dusk in the side yard.
The candles made circles of light blindness so you couldn't see
the person directly across the way. I remember seeing Dad's face
and Carl's face, but not Jack's. His voice, though, making plans,
was clear and, even in all that space and darkness, substantial.
The plan was that Jack would stay and help Carl with the har-
vest, and then we would be married. One of them took out a
wallet and a little calendar, and there was some discussion about
when the beans would be in and there was some difficulty reading the little numbers on that calendar in the candlelight, but
finally it was settled that October 16th would be the date. We'd
be married "by the book," Jack said, in town at St. Rose's and we

would have a St. Rose's procession, or "parade," as Jack said. And Dad was talking about the "big feed" we'd put on at the hotel. After that we would settle down here and maybe raise a family and live happily ever after.

"Where will you stay until the wedding, Jack?" I asked. "Shirley and the kids will be home soon." My voice sounded childish to me.

"We'll double the kids up. That's no problem," said Carl.

"He can stay in at the hotel with the other bachelors," was Dad's idea.

"He'll stay here with me," I said.

Jack was suddenly shy. "That would be neat, but . . . "

"Why not? We're grown people. We'll be married in a matter of weeks. And this is the sixties."

"It is the sixties," Jack said, "but you'd better ask your dad about that."

"I don't have to, but I will. Well, Dad?"

"You're right, Janet. It is the sixties, and you know, I don't really see the harm, though some will. Besides, it's not up to me to say. Ask Carl, here. He's your landlord. Maybe he don't want people living here in sin."

"What do you say to that, Carl?" Jack leaned on his arms, leaned toward Carl and the table lifted at my end.

When we got the table settled down, Carl stood up and poured us all some more champagne, and raising his glass, said, "My good friend, Janet, here, will stay in this house with whoever she wants to. I would like to drink to Jan. Neighbor. Tenant. Sister-in-law." And we all drank to that.

We drank to a lot more. The toasts, the voices began to seem farther and farther away. I was at their geographic center, but it was a long way to where they were on the circumference. I looked beyond them and I was silent. I was trying to imagine the circle of points in the fields around us beyond which their voices could not be heard. I was thinking of the pheasants and foxes just outside that circle.

I only remember two more things from that night: I went in the kitchen once and the cats were on the kitchen table, one on each side of the chocolate cake, eating it in their ladylike, but furtive way. And at some point in the evening I was lying on my stomach in the back yard, drunk, hanging on to the spinning earth for dear life.

I was crying. I was remembering a hot night when Joyce and Jack and Carl and I were little. I was remembering lying out in our front yard in the center of all that could possibly be of interest to me. I was remembering the close, tiny breaths of the breeze in my ears and in my hair and in the close grass. I remembered low voices on the porch, the breeze pattering the corn leaves in the field. And best of all, I heard high above me a greater wind lifting the heads of the tall trees, making the trees sail us along, making the earth feel so old, making everything seem so settled, making my size and place on the earth just right. I lay in the grass, those years ago, and watched the black treetops shifting, drifting against the dark blue sky and I felt the motion of us all – trees and me and family and farm and the warm round earth – through time. And for a while we were all moving at the same rate, together through all that was dark.

CHAPTER 8

The Wedding Procession

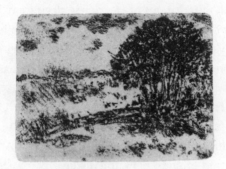

The weather was funny that fall, but then the weather is always funny, always surprises us, even farmers whose business is the weather and even flat-land farmers who can see the weather coming from a long way away.

From the end of August on until November, the trees were yellow lamps in grey light. The air was damp and heavy, a grey suspension the trees were preserved in. No wind or hard rains rushed the leaves from the trees, so for months the oaks and maples and the willows and wild cherries lit the farmhouses and the edges of the fields with yellow and rose and glowing purple. It was a good thing, too, because the sun didn't shine for weeks on end. There was fog and mist and, now and then, light rain. The ground was soggy and corn began to sprout and rot in the fields.

Because of the mild weather and all the corn not yet picked and the water standing in the fields, Canada geese, on their way south along the Mississippi flyway, took their sweet time. When you set foot outside your house that fall, you always heard the geese: the half-comical, half-sad honking, the great wings rushing the air over your head, or, almost at the edge of your earshot, their foreign conversations out in your corn. I loved to hear them and frequently hurried out of the house drying my hands to see the V's going over the yard, just as years before my mother had always rushed out to see the pipeline plane flying fast and low diagonally across Illinois. Sometimes when she had waved her white dish towel, he had dipped his wings to her.

One of Shirley's conditions for coming back to Carl was that he plant her an orchard, so one of those closed-in days before Jack and I were married, Carl and Jack and I took a truck into Bloomington and brought back the dozen trees on Shirley's list. It was decided to plant the orchard at our place – Jack's and mine – because there was the perfect spot for it and because Jack and I, not having children and not planning on any for a while would have the time to water the trees those first years. Anyway, that was Shirley's thinking; we would have trees instead of babies. Which was fine with me.

It was a comic scene – the three of us digging the holes for the little trees when each spade full of mud felt like it weighed fifty pounds, and soon our boots were weighted with another fifty pounds apiece. We worked all afternoon in slow motion, and our clothes, too, were heavy from sweat and the constant drizzle. It would have been funnier, but Jack, who in a way had no rights in the matter – the land was Carl's, the trees and the idea were Shirley's – had appointed himself in charge. Carl had a plan in mind, but Jack had a plan on paper for what tree went where and how far apart they should be and how close to the house. Carl's plan was seat-of-the-pants, but Jack had looked stuff up, so he knew about cross-pollination and pesticides and drift and the birds and the bees. So the apple trees were put in farthest from the house, because with the cherry trees near the back porch, Jack said, "she can just run out and flap her arms and scare them off." "Them" was birds. "She" was me.

Carl looked at me then; he watched my face and waited, questioning, but I said nothing, and that was one of the saw kerfs in a straight board that, added up, make it bend. I said nothing. Jack was being a jerk – to me and to Carl and to Shirley – and I said nothing, I guess, because it all felt so precarious and I was afraid of what might get said or revealed if the waters were roiled up. I felt I owed Jack everything.

After a while, it was only Jack and me planting trees, and, though Jack tried to pretend it was all still funny and jolly and so did I, we both felt awful when Carl stalked off. When we were finished, we took our wet and muddy clothes off on the back porch and stood for a moment in our underwear and sock feet looking out at our handiwork. I think we were both depressed by the greyness and the mud and those sad little sticks that were Shirley's trees. But later, in the warm yellow light after baths and after supper, we held each other in bed and watched television; we felt all right and everything was fine. Jack and I were together and nothing else mattered.

It was only a few days after Jack had proposed to me that he had moved in, so my mother and my sister went immediately to work full-tilt planning our wedding. Four or five times a day Mom would call up and ask us things like did we want ivory or white for our invitations and did we want chicken or pork roast for the dinner, but after about a week of us having no opinion or preference whatsoever, she finally said, "The hell with you! It's not your wedding anyway. Weddings are for the bride's and groom's parents." So she took it out of our hands which was fine with us. The wedding, to me, just seemed a town thing, but

Jack did want the best; he wanted the wedding by the book. Since he was sure that's what Mom wanted too, he let her take over.

Carl was to be Jack's best man, and to make is symmetrical and not hurt anybody's feelings, my sister Mary was my maid of honor. Jack and I each got in touch with some friends from our colleges – Margaret and JoAnne said they'd come to the wedding. Jack's parents, whom he tracked down in an RV camp in Idaho, said they'd be there. He found Joyce, too; she was on the road with her church group in Missouri, though after Jack talked to her on the phone, he said, "I don't know if that was a good idea or not," and he wouldn't elaborate.

The only thing I had to do was figure out what to wear. I was absolutely sure I didn't want a new dress. I wanted something that some other woman, preferably women, had worn before me. Mom had the dress that she and her mother and aunts had worn, and I wanted to wear that, though, as Mom pointed out, "It will be miles too big; you will get lost in it." So I said, "What the hell are seamstresses for?" And she said, "The fabric is too rotten to mess with, Janet!" And I said, "This one thing I want my way."

I was going on the assumption that the way to live a life was to let people have their way in everything except in the few things that you have let be important to you. Then, if you just pointed out to them that they had chosen all those other times and now it was your turn to choose, it would be clear to them and they'd say, right, it *is* your turn. I thought I could bargain that way. That's what I did with Jack. I thought all those times I deferred to his obviously strong opinion were money in the bank. I thought I could draw on them, but, of course, it doesn't work that way; Jack and I both got used to him choosing for the both of us.

In the weeks before the wedding, Jack and I seemed to live together in a house like we were twins. I was surprised by how easy it was to live with Jack. I was surprised by how fast he became necessary to me and by how happy I was living in that house with him. By the time Jack was there a week, I couldn't remember what it was like to live alone; I couldn't remember any of the advantages of solitude.

I had never dreamed that I would be so happy and that happiness would come to me from such plain things – eating breakfast with a man, painting woodwork with a man, fixing a man's supper while he watched the news. And I looked happy too. I had a good haircut finally, and I was tan and, as my Mom said, "filled out some"; everyone said I looked like a bride.

Though I, of course, loved Jack, I don't think it was romance that made me look pretty. I looked good because I knew what to do. All day long, I knew what I was to do and what to say, and not only that, I was good at it and I loved doing it. I surprised everyone, including myself. I was good at cooking and cleaning and making curtains and making do and making love and making up and making nice. I was a homemaker. Though I hadn't been aware of it, everything up to then had prepared me for this. Thinking of how close I came to not getting or taking this chance to be good took my breath away. I had stumbled, undeserving, into the chance of a lifetime.

Jack and I were both good at homemaking. Between the two of us, in about six weeks we transformed the farmhouse. We borrowed money and tools and we patched or replaced and then painted some rotten windows, broken door sills. We got rid of termites and mice. The cats were banished to the outside again, once more declared unclean. We painted the whole downstairs and put in new linoleum and bought some carpet remnants for rugs. We were so ecstatic and hard-working that everyone we knew wanted in on it, so they gave us things: Mom bought us a couch; Dad, a dining-room table and chairs. Shirley and Carl gave us a vacuum cleaner and a good mattress and box springs. Mary gave us some silverware and china. So, by the week of the wedding, we were all set up in housekeeping, and as Jack said, the only reason left to have a wedding was to get a toaster oven.

There were two rehearsal dinners – one that Mom instigated in Half Moon for all the family except Dad and his girlfriend, Marlene, and one at Carl and Shirley's in retribution for the other one. Everyone came to this one except Mom and her boyfriend, Bob, and my sister Mary, who was shocked that Dad was seeing a woman "half his age." Marlene was more than half Dad's age; two-thirds was more like it. I guess Mary thought it was OK for Mom to see Bob because he was just a harmless, ugly old church-going widower whom Mom wasn't really interested in.

Nelda and D.E. arrived home the Sunday afternoon before the wedding just as the retribution rehearsal dinner was winding down. The men were in the living room watching a football game and Shirley and Marlene and Joyce and I were doing dishes. I was drying a handful of silverware when I saw a big van swing into the driveway, so I stood in the cold fresh air of the back porch to be alone for a minute and to see who was driving in.

Things were tense back in the house. Joyce had come home, but she would not speak and the family was divided about what to do about it. Jack was furious because her "weirdness would wreck everything and why couldn't she be more considerate." The worst part was that Jack and Dad and Shirley felt free to talk about Joyce's silence in front of her as if she could not hear. Marlene and Carl said that it was none of our business and to just leave her alone, because "nobody has to talk if they don't want to." That afternoon I was too tired to express an opinion; I didn't like to think of the reasons for Joyce not speaking and I figured there was something very wrong with her, but I had a headache and an ache in my shoulders. I was tired of all the talk and the sound of the ball game and Jack's badgering Joyce and Shirley's complaining in the kitchen about Carl and his drinking; I was tired of Shirley's and Marlene's cigarette smoke; I was tired of smiling at Joyce and trying to want to be nice to this person who didn't even remind me of the old Joyce. Dad had been right about her; I'm not sure I would have recognized as Joyce Hawn this heavy, sullen woman in a dark green polyester pantsuit and bouffant hairdo. I wanted to be home alone, clean and in cold sheets, but the ball game was only half over and the dishes weren't done. And here were Nelda and D.E. driving in the driveway and I certainly wasn't ready for Nelda. I should have been preparing responses to the things she would say to make me feel small and incompetent, but all I could do was watch her and D.E. come up the back steps at me as inevitable as a cold front and then hug her with a bunch of knives in my hand. Nelda had gotten heavier on the road and so had D.E.

But, in the bright light of the kitchen, when Nelda turned around to me and hugged me to her again, very warmly, and when she held my elbows to my side and looked at my face, I was surprised to see there were tears in her eyes. "This time, no side trips to Peoria, you hear?" I heard. I nodded. I couldn't imagine why I had been such a fool of a teen-ager. This time she only said to me what I had been saying to myself.

In a little while, D.E. was settled in front of the television with a plateful of warmed-up dinner and Joyce, too, was sitting with Carl and Jack and Dad watching the game. While Shirley and Nelda went upstairs to look at Nellie whom Nelda had never seen, I sat down at the kitchen table while Marlene wiped it off. I liked Marlene. She seemed to really like my dad and I felt comfortable with her, but my eyes ached and I wanted to go home, so I put my head down on the damp Formica. After a few minutes Marlene turned off the bright overhead light, leaving on a dim one over the stove. She had been watching me and had noticed that the light hurt my eyes. I didn't say anything to her, but with my head still on my arms, I resolved to notice things about people the way Marlene did; I wanted to be as kind as Marlene was.

In a few minutes Nelda and Shirley came downstairs with Nellie. Shirley was saying that Nelda had intentionally poked the baby to wake her up and play with her. Nelda laughed and denied it and bounced Nellie around on her knee – Nellie pleased and blinking in the bright light that Shirley had turned back on. After a few minutes, Nelda was tired of Nellie and handed her over to me. Nelda got up and roamed around the kitchen opening and closing Shirley's cupboard doors, comparing them to hers: "Shirley, this is wonderful over here. I never would have thought to put cereal up here. What a good idea! What a really good idea. And so clean! I never was this clean, you know, when this was my kitchen. I never had the time. It seems there was always kids to take care of or church work to do or D.E. was wanting this or that. I never had the time to be this clean, like you, Shirley."

Poor Shirley. There was no defense against being too clean; we were all speechless in the face of this damning praise for poor Shirley, and I leaned down and gave my attention to little Nellie who was lying on my lap. She was such a pretty, new little thing and she was soon to be officially my niece. When I talked silly to her, she smiled that shiny smile babies have and reached to grab my hair with both hands and pushed her feet against my stomach. "Pretty thing," I said, "Pretty girl. Sweet girl."

I looked up when I realized the women were silent and were looking at me. I don't know why, but I blushed. At the moment Carl walked into the kitchen for more beer, Nelda said, "I just have to ask. Are you expecting?"

I could see Carl's face and he looked like someone hit him. Shirley and Nelda were watching me, and later I realized that Marlene, too, was watching Carl.

Shirley said, "Nelda, don't make the girl tell secrets she doesn't want to."

I stood up, squeezing Nellie. "I'm not pregnant. I've always been careful. I'm not. We don't want children yet; there's Shirley's trees to water." With that the women laughed, and Carl, who had been frozen with his hand on the handle, opened the refrigerator. Nelda said to me, "Relax, honey. It wouldn't be the end of the world anyway. Shirley and Carl started their family that way and, look, everything turned out OK in the end. Didn't it, Carl?"

"That's right, Mom," said Carl, now heading out the back door with his beer. But Shirley, who was sitting at the table with her feet up, called him back.

"Carl, get me one of those beers, will you?" Carl came back in the kitchen, got Shirley a beer, and went outside.

I finally drew a breath and sat down again with Nellie on my lap. I let her pull my hair over my face so no one would see that I was crying on Shirley's baby.

Marlene, all this time, was rummaging in her purse, looking for something and cursing under her breath. "Oh my god!" she said. "That does it. Who's going in town with me to get cigarettes? You are, Janet. I pick you. Let's go. Hand that baby to her grandmama. We'll be right back. Shirley, is there anything you want at the store?" Marlene was trying to rush out of there, but Shirley needed some Pampers and some vanilla or something, so while Marlene wrote them down, I went out to her car.

Carl was coming across the lot, squashing the now-empty beer can in his hands. I stood in the driveway beside Marlene's

Corvair; Carl walked right past me without looking at me or speaking. I turned to say something to him, but Marlene was coming out the door.

As she came down the steps, she said, "Carl, do you want to go in town with me and Janet and get some cigarettes? Need any beer? Those of us with vices have to pay the price to keep up our supplies." Carl was about to walk past her, too, but Marlene put out her hand to stop him. He turned and looked back at me. I saw then that Carl was dog-tired and maybe drunk and that he looked about forty years old when he was only twenty-four or so.

"No thanks, Marlene. I'll stay here, but you could bring back a twelve-pack if it isn't too much trouble." He went back in the house and Marlene and I left.

When we got to the hard road, Marlene punched in the lighter, reached into her purse on the seat between us, and got out a cigarette.

The rhythmic windshield wipers, the cold air, the relief at being out of the house with someone, for the first time that summer, who wasn't a Check or a Flaherty or a Hawn – this was what I needed.

I looked out the window at the fields. The beautiful land went past my eyes like a cool hand on a brow. Close wet trees flickered across blue far-away groves and those groves shifted to hide red farms. We were in and out of rain and sun. Patches of the land shone white and bronze while whole fields dissolved up toward the rain. The sun burned through an iron cloud and magnified, picked clean, one white farm. Tensions from the house fell away like husks. I filled up my own body again. I was feeding on the land.

Cigarette smoke. I turned to Marlene and smiled at her. "I thought you were out of cigarettes." The sound of my voice, older and lower than usual, surprised me. This was the voice I used when I told the truth, when I knew who and where I was.

Marlene said, "I *would* be out of cigarettes if I hung around *there* much longer. Never mind. A drive will do us good."

She was quiet a while and I watched the landscape, but her breathing made me think she was thinking about talking. I was feeding on all the colors in a grey landscape, on all the detail to be seen on flat land, wondering how anyone could call this boring. I was, with each breath, in the right place at the right time; I was with the right person.

Marlene began to tell me about her sister, Arlene. I turned to watch Marlene's face. She was older than I thought when I first saw her in that restaurant with Dad and another couple. I liked Marlene's broad face. I liked Marlene. She was a kind woman, but she seemed to be someone who'd never had what she wanted or needed. I hoped she wanted my dad and he wanted her.

Marlene talked as if this were the last half of a conversation we had had the first half of a few days before, but this was the first I'd ever heard of Arlene. There was some understanding Marlene was presuming I had.

"When Arlene took her kids and left Roonie, she says to me, 'Marlene, don't ever let it get so bad that you have to just walk out and leave all your dishes.' At first I thought Arlene meant leave them dirty in the sink, but what she meant was, don't let it get so bad you can't leave in an orderly fashion. She meant make sure you arrange things so you can pack up your dishes and ship them to the next place."

Marlene turned and looked at me. She smiled and, after a while, she went on.

"Arlene never really let Roonie know what was going on, so her leaving must have come to him out of thin air like a car accident does. Arlene was getting ready to leave for a long time, though. I know her and one thing I do know about her is that she is never caught surprised by something she feels. She's not like me. But I guess nothing surprises me now, nothing about myself, not since that time at dinner when I realized there I was hitting Bill on the back of the head in front of the boys." Her presumption of my understanding was beginning to make me nervous. "Bill was my first husband, my only one so far."

"It was just one more meal with not a word said. I got up to get something and he was just setting there chewing and then I was hitting him and what was happening was coming to him just as slow as it was coming to me. I was hitting him on the back of the head again and again with my hand and the kids were stopped in mid-chew to stare. Pretty soon I quit hitting him and then it all seemed so funny to me I couldn't stop laughing, though none of the rest of them thought it was funny at all. After that, it was just a matter of time."

Marlene lit another cigarette. "When I realized I was going to go, Janet, I thought I hope when I'm going through that house the last time I don't know it's the last time. I hope it comes to me when I'm out shopping. Maybe I'll be in the car driving and listening to the radio and all of a sudden I'll realize I'm on the interstate and I've just cashed a check for $400."

Marlene turned to me. "Did you know I've got two boys? Billy's fourteen and Jason is twelve. They're with their dad. That's OK. Boys need their dad and they wanted to stay on the same teams in the same school. They're good boys, though."

I looked out the window again. I realized that I doubted that they were good boys. On almost no evidence, I didn't like her ex-Bill and his sons. I realized I didn't ever want to have male children, and, come to think about it, girls didn't thrill me either.

"I don't think I want children," I said.

Marlene didn't say anything for a few minutes. "If I had it to do over again," she finally said, stubbing out her cigarette, "I wouldn't."

We were at the edge of town now, in the supermarket parking lot on a grey Sunday afternoon.

Marlene opened her door and then closed it and reached for my arm to hold me in the car. We faced each other. The window began to steam up.

"I'm going to talk plain to you, Janet, because if I don't, I won't be able to sleep with myself." She took my hand in both of hers. "You're making a mistake. The big one. I know. I've made it too. I don't know how I know, but my female intuition tells me that you are letting yourself be railroaded into something."

"Marlene! I'm happy!" I said. "I love living with Jack." My voice was the ingenue's voice again. I was receding in my body again, watching my own performance. I knew what Marlene was talking about.

"That may be true, but I still think it's a mistake. You should just run off with him."

"Oh, no," I said. "I really don't care about the wedding. I really don't. And Mom and Mary are having the time of their lives planning this wedding and running things. Jack and I don't mind at all."

" 'Jack'?" she said. "I meant run off with Carl."

I pulled my hand out of hers and shrunk back in the seat away from her.

"Janet, honey, don't be scared. I haven't and won't say a thing. Not to anybody. But I know what is going on."

"Was!"

"*Was* going on. I'm not blind. I'm the only one, though, who has no good reasons not to see it. I don't think anybody else has any idea."

"Marlene, please, I can't talk about this. Please. I love being with Jack. You don't see how important all this is . . . that Jack and I get married. I'm happy with Jack. It all makes so much sense, Jack and me." I believed myself. It did make sense.

"There's one thing you haven't said."

"I *will* love Jack. I do love him. I will fall in love with him." I was irritated then with Marlene. I didn't want to try to explain how little the way I felt now about Jack had to do with anything.

"You're right; you might. It just seems like such a long shot, Janet, such risky business." She sighed and looked out at the big windows in the front of the supermarket. "And I'm a fine one to talk, I guess." Without looking at me, she asked, "What would you think if I married your father?"

"I don't know. I don't mind. I like you, Marlene, and you're good to my dad. I guess I think it's a good idea if you're lonely and he is. If you would be happier together than alone." I told her what I thought.

She looked at me and shook her head. "You're awfully young to think like that, to think that's as much as there is." She leaned toward me and held my wrist. "Is that why you're marrying Jack?" She sat back in the seat, away from me, to get a better look at me. "You can't answer that, can you?" She laughed. "Come on, Janet, let's go get cigarettes and beer and Pampers. I just wish they sold dope in Eisners." We got out and walked arm-in-arm in the drizzle. "Wouldn't that be neat? Little packages of Acapulco Gold hanging next to the Brach's. Your dad is quite the pot head, you know."

"No! I don't believe it!"

"It's true. It's true."

Marlene and I had a fine time, but from then on we kept between us a cushion of jokes against all her unanswered questions.

When we got back to Carl and Shirley's, we found them all whooping it up in the kitchen around Dad, who was sitting at the kitchen table with his head in his hands.

"What's wrong with Dad?" I asked the jokers.

"Oh, God, everything. You won't believe it. Poor Ed!" Jack was standing behind Dad, massaging his shoulders and Dad was moaning.

"What is it?" Marlene asked more firmly.

Finally they calmed down enough to tell us that Shirley's mother had called and this is what she had heard in church this morning: My great-aunt Polly Flaherty from Iowa, who had died at the age of ninety-seven several weeks before, had left my mother everything: 240 acres in Iowa. Mom's geezer advisors in town had told her to sell that farm and invest in "urban" real estate, so Mom was buying the Half Moon Hotel where Dad was living. Dad was once again living on Flaherty property.

"I've got to get out of there and I like it there," Dad moaned.

There was some general hilarity about the long arms of the Flahertys and someone suggested that Dad's best bet was to run for President because maybe Edith couldn't buy the White House out from under him. Marlene and I smiled at each other, and she whispered to me, "I'll find a nice place for your dad where Edith can't get him."

Marlene did look hard for a place, especially after they found out that next spring that *she* was going to have a baby. Dad and Marlene were married in May and they and the little girl, Vickie, my half-sister, I have to keep reminding myself, lived together — apparently very happily — until Marlene disappeared, left with Vickie, one windy morning in March five years later.

Our wedding was a kind of high-water mark; it was a very good time, though Mom turned out to be right about the wedding-dress fabric. It was rotten, a fact which I worked hard at maintaining as a simple physical fact, not an omen, though others chose to see it as a joke or a Chinese fortune or, at the least, a good story to tell. After the ceremony, which Dad says "came off without a hitch," during the procession from the church to the hotel, either Carl or Mary stepped on the hem of my still-too-long dress. Though it was the middle of October, the weather was still unseasonably hot and sticky, and I had thought it smart to not wear stockings or even a slip, just, perversely, a pair of the yellow lace underpants I had bought earlier that summer – something neither old, new, borrowed, nor blue. So when whoever-it-was stepped on the hem of my skirt and it ripped in the back from the waistband, there was my almost bare rear-end sticking out, a sight, though split-second, not lost on the old men sitting on the porch of the hotel across the street. There followed immediate and general hilarity, which was somewhat dampened by all the women who quickly bunched around me to preserve what was left of my dignity and virtue. While my mother was proclaiming what I should have and shouldn't have done, two emergency sewing kits were produced from pocketbooks, but the fabric was too far gone for repair. Around me were concentric circles of mayhem – women, then girls, then boys, men, and old men. While I stood on that uneven sidewalk, holding my skirts tight in my arms, and, for the ladies, tried not to laugh, I was steadied by the sight of the brown fields below us, stretching away to the west from the edge of the town. Two skinny teen-aged boys were hauled over and their white patent leather belts whipped off, but both belts were too big to hold up my skirts. Someone was sent off to the hardware store for a punch to make a belt fit, and someone was looking for a Swiss army knife, but Nelda Hawn saved the day when she snatched the long white chiffon scarf from around her neck and wrapped it around my waist, and tied it tight, tight to hold up my skirt.

Jack, too was in the center of this circus, and that was the first time I ever saw him not know what to do or say or where to put his hands. When Nelda was tying my skirt up, and I had my hands on Jack's shoulders to keep my arms out of her way, I felt his arms and legs jitter as if from some little independent pains, and his mouth and stance faked, badly, tolerance and good humor. Jack was useless, embarrassed, and just plain mad. He certainly didn't, as most people did, think this funny. He looked like he would cut and run, but I held him still with my hands on his shoulders and with my smile and my eyes. Jack's eyes: I saw then that they weren't just blue; they were every color and I saw in them more than I could name, detail I had overlooked all my life, detail I realized could last me a lifetime. They would always be a place for me to look. For the first time in the twenty-two years I had known Jack Hawn, I didn't just love Jack as you love someone you admire and are used to, someone you want to be or to have. Through those cracks in his confidence and competence, I saw a way in and I saw that I would like it in there. I count my marriage to Jack from that moment. I felt bad for his confusion, but this small event – this accidental display of my lace-covered rear – let me have my first good look at Jack Hawn.

And it *was* a good story. Three or four times during the reception I heard Dad trying out various versions of the story on people who, like him, had been there.

My bride days after that were made of material new to me. They were made of a stuff I'd never felt when I was single and uninitiated, and the stuff was made of little rituals, domestic pleasures, the weaving our bodies made, long visions of the future. And my days were made of watching Jack and taking care of Jack, and of something else – fear of losing Jack. I don't know if it had taken me a lifetime or no time at all, but now I was in love with Jack Hawn.

CHAPTER 9

Along the Rock River

It was dark. My car lights shined ahead on the empty road. May sat beside me apparently looking at only what the car lights showed her – the tarred expansion joints of the road, some weeds and Queen Anne's lace in the roadside. She was a passenger, the most passive passenger. The last passenger pigeon was named Martha. I thought of this as I looked in the rearview mirror at the little heap of deer now behind us beside the road. When I was a kid I had either seen this passenger pigeon stuffed, in a museum somewhere, or else photographed just before she died. The image was very clear of this pigeon from the side, hunched down, embarrassed, waiting, but it was impossible to tell from my picture if the pigeon was alive or dead.

May sat still, looking ahead even when I put on the flashers and got out of the car. I walked shakily over to the other car where a man and a woman – faces whitened in the glare of a headlight – picked pieces of glass off the front of their car. I had seen them give the deer a glance as they got out of the car, but they didn't cross the road. As I walked up to them, they gave me merely a glance, too. "Is the deer dead?" I asked, though I knew it was. It was so still, so inanimate. They didn't answer.

"The poor little deer," I said, hugging my arms to myself.

" 'The poor deer'?" The woman bristled and they both stared at me. " 'The poor deer'? *You* done it. Your brights was on. You blinded him." She nodded her head toward her husband. "He couldn't see that deer."

It *was* my fault. My brights *were* on and I should have done something – hauled that little deer out of the road, or shoved it. I felt sick. I walked back in the direction May and I had come, towards the deer. It lay there beside the road, rearranged, now not like a deer at all. I didn't get close enough to see any details that I might not be able to get rid of.

I was shivering. My knees felt weak as I walked on the concrete back to May and my car. Grass grows in some of these cracks in the road, I noticed. May must be tired, though she looked just the same to me.

As I passed the couple, the woman crossed the road and thrust a pad and pencil in my hand. "Put down your name and address and insurance company." As I wrote, I could hear the crickets in the roadsides start up again. They knew the commotion was over.

For the second time that day, I stood for a moment with my hand on the car door handle, divided, this time not between going and staying, but three ways – between the silver shine of the Rock River beyond the trees, the dark heap back there beside the road, and a tiny, sweet sound that might be singing coming from inside the car. Without opening the door, and moving slowly so I wouldn't startle her, I bent my head down and peered in the open window. May was looking away from me and away from the river toward the Queen Anne's lace beside the road, which, in the yellow light of the flashers, seemed to be opening and closing like hands. I didn't hear the singing sound again.

As I drove off, I shut the window and, for a few minutes turned on the heater until I stopped shivering. I thought of Jack so many miles behind me. He didn't seem far away, just smaller, as though we were still in the same room and I was looking at him through the wrong end of a telescope. I knew the real distance was great, but I wished that I could reach out and touch his shoulder.

It was almost nine o'clock, so Jack would be in the living room lying on the couch watching some movie on television. I could see him in the blue light. I could reach out and feel the beer can he'd been slowly drinking from, feel where the can was warmed by his hand. If I rested my head on his chest, I could smell — beneath the scents of all the products he used on himself — his cotton tee shirt, his hair, the warmth of his neck, his sweat, his mouth. In the car I touched my mouth and remembered on it the feel of his ears, his chin. How could I have wanted to be so far from him? Jack's body was for years my farm, the hills outside my windows. Jack was what I knew of the world. He was how I knew the world; he was my means and my end. I had married him over and over; though he didn't know this, I had had to marry him over and over. As he seemed to take me farther and farther from where I wanted to be, I had married him in each new town, with each job he took on, with each new shirt and vest, with each three-piece suit and haircut and pound around his belly. All the time I was wanting to go back, he was pulling me forward into what I called the world and he called reality, progress, the dream come true. We seemed to only get farther from the farm we both wanted, from home. The Jack I had married seemed to become more and more submerged in this business man.

I thought of the winter morning just before we left Illinois for good, when everything but one thing had gone wrong. Shirley had convinced Carl that the farm really couldn't support two families, and maybe she was right. Dad had gotten Marlene pregnant and they needed a place; our place was the logical place since it was Dad's home and since they could pay rent. Carl was drinking too much, was resentful and even more incommunicative than usual. And it began to be clear that the Vietnam war, which we had all been careful to keep off our land, was disregarding our borders. It looked like Jack would be drafted. So when he was offered a job back in Madison working with his professor testing defoliants, and because, in a way, we had no choice, we decided to leave the farm. But between the time we decided to leave and the time we could leave there was a delay, a strange two months. The only ones who were nice to us were Marlene and Dad, and I couldn't be nice back to them because they were going to be the ones living in our house, Jack's house and mine.

It was the end of March and I felt a temporary reprieve from all this resentment and hostility because we were in the middle of a blizzard, a three-day blow that had cut us off from everyone and everything. This was what I really wanted, a world reduced to Jack and me, living in the ruins, in the center of a lot of flat land. I was never happier than when we were marooned alone together, no choices left, everything jettisoned, the world reduced, simplified to what seemed a manageable size. Now I know it was a child-sized world I wanted, but it took me years to see that. It was the end of March. The winter up to then had been mild, so all of Shirley's fruit trees were in bud, and now with the blizzard and the cold that we knew would follow, her first crop was lost. I am ashamed to say I was glad.

That blizzard reminded us that our old house was not that much of a shelter anymore. Rivulets of snow crept under the door in the front room, and the wind whistled through hundreds of cracks letting us know how precarious was our human purchase on the land. It was night. We were in our bedroom. Jack lay on his stomach naked in light that must have been part moonlight, part pole light, and part snow light. Jack was never cold or hot; any climate was OK with him. I sat wrapped in a blanket cross-legged beside him looking at him and looking out the window at the snow that wasn't constant but seemed to come like scarves or flocks of birds, showing us the currents of the wind. At some point in our lovemaking, Jack had sobbed, and, though he tried to disguise the sound, I knew it was a cry. Now he was quiet, facing away from me, watching the snow too. I reached out and with the tips of my fingers traced a path down the center of Jack, from the brushy hair of his head to the gentle valley of his ass. Back and forth I traced this path and felt all along him the changing qualities of warmth and terrain. Jack was very beautiful to me, the most beautiful human being I had ever seen. I looked and looked at him and traveled all over his back with my fingers. He was still dark where he was shirtless in summer and at the dip where his waist was, he whitened like bare hills do. His rear was two white hills. "It's blacker here in the bottomland," I said, my finger following his spine to the shadows between his legs. Jack was silent, but I leaned and looked at his face; he was watching the snow. My fingers traced square fields on his back, then furrows in each field. "We'll have a farm some day, Jack, one with hills, gentle hills. We'll have a farm with hills like your ass."

Jack didn't say anything for a moment. "Like my brother's ass, you mean."

Jack was facing away from me so I thought I must have mis-understood what he said. "Not like your brother's is, a better one, more beautiful."

"I didn't say my brother's *farm*. My brother's farm is as flat as your chest."

I froze there in every way and when, after how much time I don't know, I finally figured out what to say to Jack, how to ex-plain, he was asleep. I covered him up with the blanket I'd been wrapped in and got up and put on my nightgown and robe.

I went downstairs and made myself a cup of tea and sat at the kitchen table with the little lamp on, holding onto the teacup. I thought it all must be over. I'll have to leave. I knew that pretty soon I would be very sad, and perhaps angry, and lonely and a mess, but while I sat there in the middle of the night in the middle of the blizzard and the only warm spot in the world seemed to be the teacup I was holding, I felt an odd sense of relief. I truly had nothing left to lose, nothing to guard, or to take care of. That's the way I saw it then; it was freedom and purity and cleanness. I sat there without moving, and I planned exactly what to pack and what to say – very little of each – and in what direction to drive the car. Over and over I ran a silent film – me packing a small suitcase, telling Jack only that I was sorry, and going out to the car, putting my bag in the back seat, and then driving off west on a clear cold bright blue day. But I finally had to stop the movie, because anyone even as impractical as I am had to deal with the fact that the roads were drifted shut and no one was going anywhere tomorrow and maybe even the next day. I sat there a long time trying to mentally get myself out of there, but there was no way. Our road would not be plowed out maybe for days and even the big tractor could not get through the drifts that I knew must be out there. I tried to imag-ine myself walking out, but that was ridiculous. No one could come and get me. I tried the phone without knowing who I wanted to call, but the phone was dead. So, finally, because I was the only human being awake for miles, and because the wind blew so fiercely and had come from so far, and because Jack was so small in the storm and so was I, I went back upstairs and crawled under the blanket beside him, put my arm around his back, and went to sleep.

The next morning when I woke up, Jack was already up, I could smell the coffee, and the sun was dazzling. I went downstairs and there was Jack sitting at the kitchen table, opposite where I had sat the night before, and he was drinking his coffee. A cup was poured for me, but I stood beside his chair, clearly about to explain. He reached out without looking up at me and gathered my two hands in his right hand. "Janet," he said, "what's done is done. Whatever that was is behind us. Don't say anything else, please." He looked up at me sideways and looked quickly away. "Now drink your coffee," and he pushed it towards me. "Then get dressed, because we have to shovel to even get to the tractor. We've got plenty to do, Janet."

May and I stayed in the neat-as-a-pin cinder-block Ohio Motel on the Rock River. In the room were eight bouquets of plastic flowers, I counted them, and four landscape scenes on the walls. May sat down in one of the chairs by the window and looked at the green and blue sofa-sized painting of a narrow and winding valley, while I called Jack. I expected that all the love I felt for him, my newest reconversion to him, could be felt through the wires, but he didn't hear it. He went on about some idiot or other who had turned him down for a job he hadn't applied for, turned him down for the wrong job. Something had gotten screwed up in some personnel office; Jack was beside himself, so of course he couldn't take it in, even when I, acting ridiculous, said, I love you I love you I love you I love you I love you – eight or ten times until May laughed out loud. I turned to her. I said the appropriate consoling things to Jack and hung up.

"May," I said, "I love you. I love you. I love you." She laughed again, and though it sounded wonderful – deep and physical and complete like a baby's laugh – it was wrong. Her timing was wrong. I got up and held her by the shoulders and aimed her at me. "I love you I love you I love you I love you I love you I love . . . " She looked past me at the lake and birch trees scene that faced the beds. I *did* love her. I was pretty sure I did. "May, stay in this room. I'm going for a walk alone."

The soft air smelled like mud, and the river, like fields. As I walked past the office, I could see in there in the room beyond the office the manager and her husband. She was folding clothes – snapping out a pillowcase – and he was watching TV. The window was open. I tried to walk quietly on the gravel of the parking lot. There was enough light from the motel sign to see that a little path led to a lawn by the river where there were some wooden lawn chairs and a picnic table. Just beyond was the black river which I strained to hear, though for a few minutes I was afraid of it. I became conscious of the volume and weight of the water. I was afraid – as a child is – that the river might come and get me, so I said a small, dumb prayer that the law of gravity would hold while I went to sit by the river and hear what it had to say. I imagined myself there sitting at the picnic table and I could already hear the river's mutters and asides, feel the chorus of sweet nothings at my ear when a human voice from behind me turned me around. "What?" I said.

It was the manager. She was walking toward me across the parking lot. "I said, is there anything you and your mother need? How are you getting along? Is there anything I can get you?" By the last question, we were standing under the Ohio Motel sign where "vacancy" flashed off and on. The lady was little and very earnest. Though her hair was dyed bright red, she had a sweet face. She held my arm in a tight little grip. Her hair and her voice and her hand were very intense, but her face was mild and relaxed. "Have you eaten yet? Would you like to come in and join me for a cup of coffee?"

I said no, that it would keep me awake, but she said triumphantly, now gripping me with both hands, "But I have Sanka! And I have some cake." It was apparently settled, and as, arm-in-arm, we went back to her office, she asked, "Do you like your room? Is there anything you need? Is it clean enough?"

"It's the cleanest room I've ever been in," I said, and it was.

"Oh!" she said like I'd told her Paul Newman loved her. "Oh, thank you."

"I'm sorry," I said, stopping her outside her door. "I can't come in for coffee. My mother isn't well and I can't leave her alone for long."

"*I'm* sorry," she said. "But you *can* come in while I get you a kit." And she opened the screen door and I went in.

"A kit?"

"I'm Fan Butcher," she said and I followed her through her office into their living room which was a jumble, an assault of colors. "And this is Early." A big man in a dark recliner gave me a wave without taking his eyes off the TV. The room around the man seemed to be the *source* of plastic flowers. Multi-colored bouquets covered every table surface and the buffet and they hung from macrame hooked into the ceiling. Not only that but red and orange flowers bloomed on the throw on the sofa, blue flowers and pink flowers on the pictures on the walls, and pillows covered in flowers covered chairs and even leaned against the wall. I stood square in the center of a gold flower on the red carpet while Fan looked for something in the room beyond.

In a few minutes, Fan came back, still talking, but I hadn't been listening. "Here's your kit for you and your mom. I just had to put a couple of things in."

"Kit?" I asked again.

"For my *nice* guests," she said, bowing a little and handing me a little basket with a handle. "If I know they're nice folks, I like to make them at home. Take this back to your room. It's all for you," she said. I must have looked like I couldn't believe my fortune. "Keep everything in it, take it with you. Just think of me." Her moist hands pressed hard the backs of my hands which were on the handle of the little basket. I felt the wicker snap in my hands, but she didn't seem to notice.

"Thank you, Fan," and for a frightening moment I thought I was going to cry, but I didn't and when I turned to go, Early gave me the same backhand wave and again no glance. That man – Early Butcher – was the most out-of-place man I'd ever seen. In his dark clothes on that dark recliner in the center of that bright room, he looked like something waterlogged that had sunk to the bottom of a crowded aquarium.

Fan and I walked outside together and I told her that I *would* come back and I *would* tell all of my nice friends about this wonderful, clean, homey motel and then I asked her why it was called the Ohio Motel. Years before it had been the Rock-A-By Motel.

"Because I'm from Ohio," she said, "the prettiest little valley. A place much older than this, a place settled more than 150 years ago, and I thought if I called it Ohio I'd make myself think I was home. A *real* river ran through that valley, with two waterfalls and clear water. Not like that stuff out there." She let go of my arm to wave with real contempt toward the river.

Unhitched from her, I told her I had to go see about my mom, who'd had a stroke, I found myself saying, and couldn't talk. She couldn't ask for anything herself, I explained, and I had to see if she needed anything. Then Fan smiled at me with tears in her eyes and pushed me and the basket away from her, toward my duty, my mother, toward Ohio, I think.

Fan Butcher stood in the lighted doorway of her home away from home and watched me until I got to the door of our room. I turned and waved at her and went in.

May was sitting on the edge of the bed, and she was on edge, waiting. When I went in she, as usual, didn't smile or greet me, but she did seem to stop waiting.

I got May washed and undressed and in her nightgown and then I turned back the spread and tucked her neatly in the bed. As I was brushing my teeth, I stepped out of the bathroom once to check on May and realized that, other than the fact that I had to dress and undress my roommate, these cement block walls and the narrow and thin beds and the silence of the other female made me feel just like I was in college again. I liked it like this. I wished I hadn't complicated the air in the room by trying to tell Jack how much I loved him. At that moment, standing in the bathroom doorway looking at the old woman who was looking out the window toward the river, I was happy with this. I was happy being just a woman who took care of things – any woman who took care of any other woman and again I thought of the now-baby who would some day take care of me. "Listen," I told her out loud. "Don't get rid of my stuff. Steal it or take it home or give it to someone you tell about me." I then realized that I really didn't have any stuff; I had been getting rid of everything, trying to travel as light as possible for years. I would have to start saving some woman stuff. All I had was some of the blue canning jars that were my grandmother's.

I put on my nightgown and turned off the TV and the air conditioner and the light and opened the curtain and the window and got into bed. We couldn't hear the river or see it, but after a while I could feel a little of its air on my face. But May lay there so tense I thought she might clap shut like a tight book. At first I thought she was looking out the window, but I slowly realized that what I thought was her hair was her pale face and she was looking at me with some kind of accusation. She seemed to feel that the light which landed on her was some kind of imposition, an indignity I forced upon her. Or maybe it was the dark or the silence or the air from the river. Or the chain on the door or the chair propped against it to keep old ladies from roaming. In any case, I turned on the bedside lamp and turned on the TV low and got out of bed and, pushing her legs to one side, sat down beside her on her bed. "May," I said, "your friend and mine, Fan Butcher, has given us this little basket of things. She calls it a 'kit.' Let's see what it is." I set the basket down between us on the bed and May sat up and drew her legs under her. She wanted to see what was in the basket that looked like the one that Little Red Riding Hood took to her grandmother's – red-checked cloth and all. I spread the cloth – a remnant pinked at the edges by Fan herself – between May and me on the bed and took out the contents and laid them out on the cloth. There was a tiny pad of pastel notepaper, a package of Clorets, some Wash-N-Dri, a paper of little gold safety pins, some packets of Sanka and sugar and Sweet 'N Low, an Eversharp, and a box of chocolate-covered cherries. There was one of those accordion-fold plastic rain hats and a collapsible drinking cup with roses painted on it. At the bottom was a Polaroid photograph of Fan Butcher standing in front of her Ohio Motel and some business cards:

THE OHIO MOTEL

Fan and Early Butcher
Owners and Managers

"We'll take care of you like family."

Someone walked past the window, paused, and then walked back. It was Fan. I would recognize that needy step anywhere. Before she came back, I turned off the TV and the lights and got back in my own bed with a couple of the chocolate-covered cherries. I didn't want to talk to her, but it was nice to know she was out there. I was here by the big, thick river and one funny lady was looking out for me out there and another was lying in the other bed sounding exactly like my old college roommate, Mary Jean, who used to eat in bed every night with the lights off. Like a little mouse, May rustled through the treasures on the bed, put them in the basket, dumped them out again. As I went to sleep, I was far from Jack. I was far from the dead little deer and my guilt for its dying. I was far from being a helpless old lady and I was far from being a lustful, ignorant girl. I was far from anyone's home and anyone's idea of home. I was here in the middle, for a moment safe in sleep by the Rock River in Ohio in Illinois.

I dreamed of a hill farm. I dreamed myself walking on a path on the side of a steep hill covered with grasses and alfalfa. From there I could see a long way up and down the valley. I could see all the land that was mine and I could see farms that were my neighbors' too. I was carrying something, I was working, I was happier than I'd ever been. I could see a long way.

Sometime around dawn, I half awoke to see a woman in a chair by the window bent over her sewing in the pale light. In my mind it was Grandma Check and I was a child with a fever. I went back to sleep and the sleep under her watchful eye was sweet and deep. When I woke again I was all in working order — clear headed and clear sighted, and that is perhaps why what I saw next was so upsetting: I knew I was seeing well and thinking well and not making things up, but for a few moments I still couldn't put it all together.

What I saw was May sitting in the chair by the window — just sitting in the chair and looking out the window. She was there in her pale yellow nightgown, but she was covered with moths. Various-colored pale moths had lighted on her gown and, like a flower pattern, covered the front of her and her lap and her left sleeve. Pale pink- and green- and blue-winged things on May. I got out of bed with my heart beating so hard. I went to her quietly and none of the moths moved. I lowered myself carefully down on May's bed beside the chair and leaned to her to look.

It wasn't moths. It was little pieces of paper. The pastel notepaper from Fan's kit and the little gold safety pins. I leaned closer. There was tiny writing on the papers. "May, what is this?" I said. I took her hand and she turned from the window and looked at me and smiled. But she didn't know what I meant. I pointed to the little papers on her lap. "What are these?" She looked at where I pointed, but didn't see what I saw. She looked out the window again.

When my hands had stopped shaking enough, I unfastened one of the safety pins and read what was written on the pink paper. "Molasses" it said. I unfastened another one. "One girl Katherine." And another one. "Joe is dead." "Waldorf salad." "Two houses, white and brown." "Pond's Cold Cream." "July." "the green flowered plates." And one of the pieces of paper: "Janet Hawn takes care."

I didn't know what to think. I took all of the papers off May and saved them in an envelope. Some of them had nothing written on them. I decided not to think about this just yet. I got us dressed and packed and loaded the car. When I paid the bill, Fan pressed on us a bag of still-warm muffins, and we left before the mist had risen from the river.

The Cabbage Man

I had told May's daughter we would arrive in the afternoon – "definitely not before lunch" – I had said on the phone. We had eaten breakfast and were on the road before it was even eight o'clock, but it was less than a two-hour drive to Quincy. Because I didn't want to call May's daughter and change our plans and because I wanted May to myself a little longer, I turned right the first chance I got and drove due west on little roads until we got to the Mississippi River.

The river was wider than I remembered and excited me more than I thought it would. It appeared and disappeared from me often as I drove along the Great River Road – here, it glittered beyond some woods like a great song; there, the story of your life beyond a row of houses on the bluff. I stopped at a supermarket and bought May and me a few groceries. A perfect summer day. People walking slowly on the streets of the little town looked like they felt on their faces this blessing – a sunny Sunday morning in June. At the edge of the same town, I found a park that overlooked the river. May and I would spend the morning here. "Mississippi" was the one word she'd said to me in more than a year; this must mean something to her, and maybe it will come back to her. Maybe she will tell me. Maybe she will explain her moths.

And I wanted to think about something; I wanted to look at something that is harder to remember than the distant past. Thinking about the things I did and didn't do when I was a girl was easy enough; I could almost disown her, she was in so many ways unlike me. Thinking about what I did and didn't do last year was a different story. I woke up this morning seeing so clearly from that dream hillside overlooking that little dream valley. I woke up knowing what it felt like to have clear sight. I would sit here on this hillside overlooking this wide, wide valley and river and I would remember what happened to Jack and to me last year. I would, for the first time in six or eight months make myself remember the cabbage man. I would carefully try to see what happened.

May sat on the blanket beside me in the dappled shade of a locust tree. She put things in and took them out of the basket that Fan gave us. I could smell the river, or the wet rotting parts of Illinois that lined its bank, but I could not see it in the sense that you see water moving south; the effect of it was more like the effect of light on me; in fact, right after we got there I had to walk down to the shore and squat down and put my hands in it to make myself believe it as a river or even a body of water instead of just a great glare between here and the grey-green bank that was Iowa. I sat and looked at Iowa, wondering how much, to someone on the other side, this bank looks like that one does from here. I don't think there is in the world that kind of symmetry really, but it is tempting to imagine things that way – that on the other side are people looking at us look at them and what they see is what we see, so that somewhere in the world is the same view as the one from your head, but I think there is no reciprocity in views and that is perhaps what all of this is about, why all this happened.

"Madam, is this your cabbage?" That started it.

One Sunday morning a year ago last March, I went out to buy groceries for the week, but I just didn't have the nerve, I guess, so I pushed the cart up and down all the aisles, bought a cabbage, and then I walked across the street to church. I hadn't been to Mass in years, so I was surprised that the church was packed, standing-room only, and that the Mass was a teen-aged one with guitars, banners, and a slide projector showing pictures of local teen-agers and daisies. But Mass is Mass, so I stood in the back with my cabbage, sweating in my coat on that very warm March day. While they were singing "Wasn't That a Time," I dropped the cabbage which I had nervously twisted up in its brown bag, and it rolled behind me somewhere. I couldn't really look for it as the people were packed in there so tight I couldn't see the floor, and I certainly couldn't lean over and feel around. I thought I'd ignore it until Communion, but after a few moments I heard this mock-serious male voice behind me say, "Madam, is this your cabbage?" He asked again and I turned around, which is as odd as facing backwards in an elevator, and saw my cabbage thrust out to me between the people behind me who looked at that cabbage like it was something about to go off. I traced from the hand it was held out in back to the face of a middle-aged man with very blue eyes. He looked amused.

I reacted so slowly there among the Catholics packed in like trees that he had to ask me a third time: "Madam, is this your cabbage?" Finally I said, "Yes, I think so," which was not too bright, but he signalled me with a nod to follow him out of church and get my cabbage.

I am too slow. That's what Jack always says. "Can't you tell what you think when you think it? How can you *not* know what you feel? How can you *not know* if you like or don't like someone? React!" I decided as I followed the cabbage man (I already called him that in my head) out of church that I liked his face, his eyes, and his enjoyment of saying in church, "Madam, is this your cabbage?"

We met outside on the steps of the church – an old, German, stone church on a high, gentle hill – and we stood blinking and gazing a moment in the March sun at the warehouse super-market across the four-lane road, the shopping center, and the rank upon rank of condominiums on the hills beyond. This little farming town had been overrun years before by the city, but the curve of these hills was still wide and dramatic; it was too bad the only dramas played out here were commercial ones. Even this church was for sale; the parish was going to build a more energy-efficient church and school. I stood beside this man I hadn't yet spoken to and thought it must have been good fifty years ago to be a bride setting out from these high steps with a wide valley, fields, and pastures all before you. You could go a long way in a marriage with this place as your beginning.

"How did you know it was a cabbage?" I asked before I looked at him. He wore a blue windbreaker and was only a little taller than I am, but much broader.

"I'm in produce. I *was* in produce. When *they*," and he nodded toward the warehouse supermarket across the highway, "bought A&P out, I was 'not rehired,' as they say. I was too old and too expensive for them."

Then I looked at him and saw on his face the same kind of wear that I saw on Jack's – fatigue that doesn't come from work, combined with anger, self-doubt, and thinning hope. What could I say? I knew because of Jack that there was nothing to say. Then I told him what I had just thought about how all this must have looked at one time and the effect a place like this – a "land of dreams" – could have on brides and grooms.

He said a bitter thing, really the only bitter thing I ever heard him say. He said he guessed I was right, that *land* for the people who came before us *was* the dream, "but now, the land of dreams – you're looking at it. That's what they want and that's all they'll get." And I looked out over the highway and discount stores, the vast shopping center at the bottom of the valley, the fast-food row going over the hill, and the new apartment buildings and condominiums (I lived in one of them; worked in another) on the side of the hills beyond. What I thought was how lovely it is at night, and I thought the farm-girl part of me can hate a town in the daytime, but I'm still a sucker for the "pretty lights" at night. I told him this and he asked, "Farm girl?" in a nice way that made me look at his face again. This man hadn't lost his sense of humor. Jack had.

"Where do you want to go have coffee?" I asked and thought of Jack. See, Jack, I told him in my head, how fast, how spontaneous.

"McDonald's drive-up," the cabbage man said. "Let's drive a while. Drink coffee and drive. Calms me down."

"I should be back in an hour or so."

"So should I. My name's Russell Bourget."

"I'm Janet Hawn."

"Pleased to meet you, Janet Hawn."

We took his car, got the coffee, if you want to call it that, and we drove due west away from the city on a two-lane road. That was what I did alone sometimes; I got in the car and drove west until it was far enough and something changed in me, I got some generosity again, and then I turned around and came back. I think I drove to get out of range of Jack, away from him so I could choose to go back to him. I thought I knew what the cabbage man was doing, and I thought of the blackbirds beside the road who, in pairs or in flocks, wordlessly head in the same direction for the same reason.

Beside Russell Bourget's left hand there was a plastic holder for his coffee cup. He must go out and drive a lot. He drove with two hands until we had passed the outskirts, then, when the road was a country road past only orchards and dairy farms, he took the plastic top off the coffee cup, slowed down, drove with one hand, looked at me.

At that moment, I heard Jack's voice in my head, and only then did it occur to me that, in spite of this man's sense of humor, the neatness of his car and his person, his being an overweight, middle-aged, unemployed produce manager, he might be a murderer or a rapist.

I looked at his face again. The irises of his eyes were not just blue, but a mixture of light, metallic colors. The planes of his face were broad, but there was a twilight under his eyes. His brown hair was neatly combed in front, but the hair on the back of his head gave him away. It stuck out, needed attention. This man was too tired to murder anybody or rape anybody or even conceal those impulses. I was safe with him.

Too safe, maybe. And I was tired, too.

I switched instantly from the thought that maybe this man was going to kill me to feeling that he was a dream come true. Not a romantic dream. This unemployed produce manager was no dream boat, but he seemed like someone who would listen, someone to whom I might be interesting. Though he hadn't said much since we left McDonald's, he looked at me often. (Like my dad and like Jack, he had a farmer's ability to go straight down the road without looking ahead.) What I saw in his face — curiosity, amusement, patience — made some rusted, braking ratchet inside of me begin to slip, and I began to talk.

He drove and I talked about Jack. I told him how Jack and I grew up as neighbors and that our marriage felt almost inevitable; I told him about how we planned to live in the house I grew up in all our lives and farm there with his brother; I told him how we left the farm and have been working ever since to get money to farm again; I told him about Jack's pride that would not allow him to speak to his brother who "tricked him out of his inheritance," or work as a tenant farmer, or work without comment for idiots. It was Jack's pride, as well as the economy, that caused us to move from job to job and state to state. And it was partly both of those that caused me to go to nurse's training because I couldn't think of anything else I could count on doing no matter where Jack's job took us.

The cabbage man drove west out of town for about thirty miles, through several kinds of farming country – prosperous dairy farms on the high flat plain above the bay, some turf farms in black-land valleys which were at one time lakes, and then smaller, poorer farms cut out of forest land, farms where you knew the farmer and his wife both had to have three other jobs to keep those old barns from falling in on themselves.

For years it had been all right, really, with Jack and me because he always saw that just around the next corner was the dream come true. He was amazing. Whenever he quit or was fired from a job, this released in him the most incredible hope and optimism and details of dreams. For years, those were the best times – when Jack was between jobs, when the dream was not limited by the day-to-day, by the figures on the current pay check, by the idiocies of his current boss. It was only in the cracks between jobs that our daydream seemed to bloom. And I told the cabbage man that secretly I was afraid that Jack's real skill in life was not as a man who carried out plans, but as a man who could sell you the-way-things-will-be. Jack was good at getting jobs, at the looking and the organized selling of his idea of himself; he was not nearly as good at holding a job.

He had started out in school studying ag management, then

worked for a professor of his in Madison who was a chemist, then worked for chemical outfits like Dow who found out fast that Jack was best at selling his visions to others; this became over the years pure sales and now Jack is a salesman who has sold almost everything, drugs for Squibb and machine tools and farm machinery, you name it. About four years ago, hopelessness for Jack began to switch to times of unemployment rather than employment. His own dream had become less real to him, I think, than the dreams of other men, so now he looks forward to being handed what to sell, what to be enthusiastic about.

But I was very worried about Jack. It had been a year and a half since he'd worked. He still did everything right when he looked for work: he wore the rights suits and had the right resume and the right answers in the interviews, but now there was a darkness in the skin under his eyes, a dark undertone in his voice, a helplessness in the gestures of his right hand that no American company would want anything to do with. And he was too old. He was forty-four.

The cabbage man laughed when I told him that, watched the road ahead and laughed. I realized that he must be ten years older than Jack. I couldn't think about that. "I am married to a man named Jack Hawn," I said, "but the Jack Hawn I used to know won't speak to me. Every morning this Jack Hawn gets up, showers, shaves, dresses as though for work, watches the 'Today Show,' but he doesn't talk to me and he doesn't want me to talk to him. Then he sits at his desk and he makes lists and phone calls and types up letters. I leave for work (I was working a day shift then) without talking to him. I think he waits for the mail, then takes his briefcase and goes out. I don't know where he goes; I hope it's to interviews or a mistress or a ball game. I don't care where he goes as long as he gets there what he needs so Jack Hawn will come back to me. I miss Jack Hawn."

The cabbage man said, "Tell me about your farm, about where you and Jack grew up."

After driving west for a long time on the two-lane road, the cabbage man had turned north on a little blacktop, gone about three more miles, then stopped. At first, I thought he stopped because I was crying. When he parked the car by the road, he brought a box of Kleenex out of the back and patted my shoulder in a respectable way. He had parked at the end of a long lane that led to an empty house. Curious cows came to the fence to look at the car, but after a while, pulled their hooves out of the sucking mud and moved on.

I told him one of my favorite stories about Jack and the Hawns – one that I'd heard from every point of view on the farm – from Jack and D.E. and Nelda and Joyce and Carl and from my dad's reconstructed all-seeing point of view.

One fall morning years ago when Jack and Carl and Joyce were teen-agers, Nelda Hawn was on her hands and knees washing her kitchen floor. She heard the back door open and shut, then the kitchen door open, so she looked up a little to see which one of them it was. What she saw first was a man's work shoes. But what she saw next was a man's bare white legs. What she saw after that made her faint. It was a naked man smeared with blood. It was her husband, D.E. He was standing there in her kitchen on her clean wet floor with nothing on but his work shoes and his leather belt. Not even his hat. His mouth was grinning in a new, nervous way and he was giggling, which was not something D.E. Hawn was noted for doing. His face was white as a sheet and there was blood smeared on him from the cuts and scratches all over his body. It took just a few seconds of seeing this to make Nelda pass out cold on her wet floor. Now, D.E. either figured that the cold water Nelda was lying in would bring her around, or he didn't figure anything at all; in any case, he stepped over her and began to walk back through the house to get some clothes to put on.

This scene had not taken more than a few seconds and no words had been said. But, from almost the beginning of it, Joyce, who was down in the basement ironing, knew something was wrong. It was the fact that her mom and someone else were in the kitchen without talking and it was the small, but unfamiliar, sound above her of a body falling limp onto the linoleum that made Joyce stand still and listen for the predictable, familiar sounds to begin. They didn't. There was no talk, and only one person creaked the floor above her. She took the stairs in about three steps and was in the kitchen in seconds.

Joyce has never said, but she must have both known and not known that the naked man walking away from her through the dining room could not have so quietly killed her mother, who she thought was dead on the kitchen floor. She must have known and not known that the naked man was her father and that her mother was breathing there on the floor. But what Joyce chose to know was that her mom was dead and that the naked, bloody man killed her. She too stepped over the body, and her hand closed around the most murderous thing in the kitchen – a butcher knife.

At the time all the action in the house began – when D.E. opened and closed the back-porch door – Jack and Carl were running full tilt across the lot. Before that, they had been at the corn dump dumping another wagon load of corn into the crib. They both looked up when they saw their dad's truck pull into the yard and already they knew something was wrong. He wouldn't have come in unless the equipment broke down. So Jack was reaching to switch off the dump when he saw that his dad getting out of the truck was stark naked. And when they saw that he still had on a leather belt and was bloody, they both knew without a word that he had gotten a sleeve caught in the augers on the picker and that the machinery had ripped every shred of cloth from his body.

When Joyce put her hand around the knife, Jack and Carl were almost to the back door. And when the knife was flying through the air, Jack was in the kitchen wondering will it hit Pop and Carl was wondering is she dead.

The knife did hit D.E. It gave him a good slice across his right buttock, about twelve stitches worth. Then Jack hit Joyce. He punched her in the mouth like a man slugs another man, and she dropped like a knocked-out cowboy to the wet floor. Nelda woke up when Carl clapped her a little on both cheeks like they do in the movies to get the girl to come to. Then Jack ran and got the afghan off the couch and wrapped up D.E. who was standing in the living room not understanding any of this. He took D.E. to the car, laid him down on his stomach in the back of the station wagon. Then Jack ran back for a dish towel for a compress for his dad's rear end, and to get Nelda who was crying in Carl's arms, and for Joyce who was real quiet holding her jaw, sitting in mop water. Jack put Carl in the back of the car with his dad and he had him hold the dish towel hard there to stop the bleeding. Joyce and Nelda rode up front with Jack, and until they got about three miles from home and Nelda asked what happened, not a word had been said from the time D.E. got out of the truck naked, except by Carl who said, "Mom, Mom," as he slapped Nelda awake.

The cabbage man loved that story and during the time I knew him, made me tell it to him four or five times. I told him a lot of things during those few months, but it seems like I told most of it that first day.

When he started the car and we headed back, I saw that we were in the middle of beautiful farming country. Old farmsteads with lots of outbuildings stood in front of groves of walnut or oak; some were prosperous and clean, but others were falling in on themselves. These were dairy farms. Three-quarters of a mile back the way we came was another big German church on a hill; at its feet were the rectory, a gas station, a tavern and three or four houses. This was beautiful country.

On the way back, Russell told me that he came from a farm too, about a hundred miles north of here, but a small farm, a "chicken-scratch" he called it. He told me that he had nine brothers and sisters and they were alike as "peas in a pod." It must have been a struggle making a living for twelve people on land like that, but he didn't say much about it. He told me about a horse they'd had, Nancy, a sorrel with a white blaze. All the kids in the neighborhood came to ride her because she was so sweet and gentle. "You could ride her without a saddle or a bridle; all you had to do almost was tell her where you wanted to go. But when she was tired of you, she'd run you under the clothesline and knock you off."

He said their farm and Nancy were sold a long time ago to a neighbor, but once, after he was married he drove up there with his two little boys. "I drove up to the old pasture and parked the car and got out and there up at the top of the hill with the cows was Nancy. She must have been twenty-five years old. I called to her. 'Na-a-a-a-ncy!' And she turned and came down to me there at the fence."

The cabbage man and I began to meet on Sundays — at the back of the church, as if by accident. We never talked about this; we didn't *conspire* or anything like that. We would each just sit or stand in the back, and when the other came in, we would quietly leave together. All this was wordless — as if that made it innocent. We went to one of our cars, got fast-food coffee and drove to the same place, that abandoned farm, usually with me talking the whole way.

After we had driven out there about four times, Russell told me that *this,* and he meant the empty house with its small oak grove and the barn next to it, the pasture and sloping fields beyond, was his dream. He was going to buy this farm. They (he and his wife, Loretta) could raise almost everything they'd need, he said, and he would grow some specialty produce and sell direct to supermarkets in the city. He told me that he spent his waking hours trying to figure out how to finance buying this 180 acres. He said it was next to impossible. "*Next* to," he emphasized, "*not* impossible. I know it's up a steep hill, this effort, and all the traffic is in the other direction, but I am going in this with my eyes open."

I thought, and kept it to myself, that it *was* impossible, and didn't we know it, and my heart sank for him. Something about "going in with my eyes open" reminded me of the old man I took care of. I told the cabbage man that day about the old man.

The old man had made a great deal of money – in scrap metal, he told me – so he could afford three shifts of RNs to come into his home to take care of him. I worked first shift weekdays. It was very convenient for me because he lived in a condominium just like ours four blocks away. His name was Jackson Maclean. He was ninety-eight, dying, and I thought I could, at that time, trace in the air the descending curve that was the old man's life. I could see it. I think he could too. He had a sweet smile, as sweet a smile as you can have when there is almost no flesh between skull and skin. His eyes were the milky blue and white of childhood's skies, and he was as sweet-smelling as a child. I knew his body better than anyone's; I knew I would miss it. He spoke little. Most of the time he slept in the hospital bed in the den off the dining room. There was not much I had to do but watch him sleep. When the sun was in the den in the mornings, the old man's big grey cat slept beside him, and, in the afternoons, when the sun was in the living room, the big cat, Tom, sat beside me on the couch. Both mornings and afternoons I watched through the open door the old man sleep.

All this I told the cabbage man, and I even told him some of what I imagined. I told him that one morning as Mr. Maclean lay sleeping and as I was watching him through the open doorway, I realized that the doorway and the two others beside it were like picture frames, three in a row. It was like a tryptich.

There was the old man in the first frame. The white bed and the tan carpet filled the bottom half of his picture. Above that the old man's head, chin pointed up, was surprisingly dark against the white sheets, and beneath his blue-veined hand, the grey cat slept in a ball. Beyond the bed, framed by a window, was a rosebush full of the twitter of sparrows.

Slowly, in my mind's eye, I put my husband in the second frame, the doorway to the bedroom. I saw him in profile, seated in a chair, his arms crossed on his chest, waiting.

I told Russell Bourget all this, but when he asked who was in the third frame, I didn't tell him. I didn't think it was proper, I guess.

He, the cabbage man, was in the third frame. His bulk filled the doorway, facing me, always holding out toward me my cabbage twisted in its sack. He was smiling, Jack was waiting, and the old man said *ah* as he slept.

The spring and then the summer went by quickly. I was driving out almost every week with the cabbage man. I never mentioned it to Jack, and occasionally this bothered me, but I knew I had done nothing wrong. Russell and I just drove and talked and not even a glance was improper. I had done nothing to hurt Jack. As a matter of fact, things were better between Jack and me. Because of the cabbage man, I had more patience with Jack, more understanding. If I had told Jack, something complicated would have been made of nothing. I just wasn't sure that I could explain those drives, that talk in such a way that Jack would see how simple it all was.

One Sunday evening, near the end of the summer, Jack and I almost had a big argument. It started out to be about my uniforms; it was funny, as all those fights are. I was in the living room ironing one of my starched cotton uniforms. Jack was lying on the couch, watching a ball game, drinking a beer.

"You know, there's wash-and-wear," he said.

"I know that, Jack."

"Then, why go to all that trouble?"

I thought a few minutes. "Out of respect, I guess."

"Respect for who?"

"These are Mr. Maclean's last weeks."

"What does cotton or nylon have to do with that? It's irrelevant."

"Nothing I do is irrelevant to him. The two other shifts and I are his whole world, the whole population of his whole world."

"What can that have to do with cotton or nylon? The amount of time that ironing takes you has to do with *my* world."

"These aren't your last days," I snapped, and scared myself.

"How do you know? You can't know, can you? You never know, these might be your last days." There was no threat on his face or in his voice, just the same undifferentiated anger.

I said, "If these are my last days, then I want to wear these uniforms. And besides, I told you, my arms, my skin and voice are his only human contact, mine and the other nurses."

"You talk like it's sex." He was sitting up now. I was still ironing. "You talk like you're fixing yourself up for him. You don't do that for me."

"Jack, I know where this is leading. Don't." I put the iron down. "We've said these things a hundred times. It's your fault we don't anymore, just as much as mine. It's the times, Jack, it's what we're going through. It's the worry."

I turned off the iron and hung up the uniform. "Let's go out and eat tonight. We haven't done *that* for ages, either. Come on, Jack, let's go out and try to have a nice time. Come on, Jack Hawn." I was kneeling next to him. "We'll buy each other beers and talk mushy over some four-dollar hamburgers and who knows what might happen later."

So we went out to eat. We went to one of those "family fun" steak places on fast-food row, because that's all we could afford and it was close.

It was a nice time, really – the first in a long time. We talked to each other, held hands, drank a few beers, ate cheap steaks. After dinner and after we'd ordered coffee, Jack got up to go to the john. I sat at the table waiting for him, staring out at the sunset.

The western sky framed in the restaurant window was a combination of colors that I have never seen in the country and never gotten used to in the city – dark blue at the top, a mustard color at the bottom, and electric blue in between. That sky hangs over only American cities, I'm sure, and those colors come only from money, from gases given off at the exchange of money for goods.

I was watching the sky when someone hit me on the back of my head. It was a tiny old lady in a pale blue pantsuit who walked all along the row of tables by the windows whacking the patrons with her pocketbook. Then she started down the other side whacking those patrons too. It was startling, and embarrassing for the young couple who came running after her, but it was harmless and also funny. When I turned around to see if Jack was coming back to see any of this, I saw the cabbage man at another table smiling at me. He got up and came over just as Jack sat down again.

"I remember you," he said. "You dropped your cabbage in church." Again, without talking about it, I knew what he was doing.

"Yes," I said, "and you so graciously picked it up for me. I'm Janet Hawn and this is my husband, Jack."

Then he introduced himself to both of us, and asked us to bring our coffee and join him and his wife, and he gestured back toward their table. Loretta was turned around watching all this and she too beckoned us to sit with them.

Loretta was a lot older than I expected her to be. She had an open, neighborly face that I liked right away, but seeing her entirely grey hair made me realize that Russell did something to his to make it darker, for the job interviews, I figured.

When we sat down, Russell told the story about the cabbage, about how we met, told it as if nothing had gone on after that. When he told the cabbage story, he was funny.

"Imagine," he said, "I'm in church praying to God to give me a job, when I feel something bump my foot. So I look down to see what it was and there's this brown paper bag, and, when I pick it up, I realize it's a cabbage. It's a sign from God direct to me, the ex-produce man. A cabbage. How thoughtful of God. And I wondered how God got me this job. God must know somebody. Ahead of me I notice the back of a dark-haired woman and she looks embarrassed. You know, you can see it even on the back of her neck. I think maybe she brought this sign from God, so I ask her, though there are people all around us, 'Is this your cabbage?' "

I broke in. "You said, '*Madam*, is this your cabbage?' "

"Well," he said, "I wanted to be on the formal side, considering who it was that sent you. But I had to ask you three times — just like somebody in the Bible had to ask somebody something three times. You were praying so hard, I hated to interrupt. Out on the church steps, you said, if I remember correctly, that the church would be a wonderful place to be married. 'Married?' I'm thinking. It's a *job* I want; I've *got* a wife. But who am I to argue with God. Now here you are again, so tell me which it is." Russell leaned forward on both arms and looked right into my eyes. "Do you want me to marry you or do you want me to work for you? I'll do either."

Jack was actually laughing. So was Loretta, and so was I, though Russell had taken my breath away for a moment with his question. The whole evening was like that. Loretta, in her raspy, warm, no-nonsense voice, asked for our life story practically, and she got it. Loretta was wiry and strong-looking, someone whom not much was put over on, but we felt at ease with her and Russell. Jack and Russell told farm and unemployment jokes and laughed until there were tears in their eyes. "What did the old farmer say when asked what he would do with the million dollars he'd just won in a lottery? 'Well,' he said, 'I reckon I'll just farm till it's all gone.' "

Before this evening, I had never really looked at the cabbage man while I talked to him, and I found that I liked looking into his eyes and feeling his smile on my face. The four of us ended going for drinks together after we left the restaurant. By the end of the evening, we were all fast friends with plans for other evenings.

There were many evenings together in the next few weeks. The four of us got along so well. Knowing Russell and Loretta changed things so much for Jack and me. The tight world we'd narrowed ours down to expanded. Some pressure across my shoulders relaxed, and I suspect that was true for Jack, too. Though old Mr. Maclean was near death, and though Jack didn't get a job and neither did Russell, that was almost a happy time.

On the first day of September, Mr. Maclean died. He died at the end of third shift, at six in the morning, so when I got to work, the doctor had already left and the ambulance was there to take the body to the morgue. I took care of the few things left to do, made a few calls to relatives out of state, but my main job was to find the cat. The niece told me, when I asked, to take him to the Humane Society, but I knew he was my cat now, if I could just find him. He must have been hiding from death or from all the strangers in the house, but finally I found him behind a stack of towels in the linen closet. He was waiting for me there in the dark, his eyes shining like silver and gold. I picked him up, locked the door, and left.

Jack was gone when I got home. When I put Tom down in our place, he walked all around, went in the den, and sat down in the sun as if to say, this will do just fine.

Seeing Tom there in the same place he would have been at Mr. Maclean's made me realize how upset I was at Mr. Maclean's death. I knew that it was my job to take care of the old and the dying, and therefore I shouldn't take it so personally, but I would miss him and I would miss being in his house.

I left Tom perfectly happy there on the couch. It was only ten-thirty in the morning. I decided to go for a drive.

Since Jack and I had been seeing so much of the Bourgets, I had met Russell only twice at church to drive out into the country. And I didn't like it either time. Something had changed. He was still the perfect gentleman, and I said and did and even thought nothing I was ashamed of, but because it was such a different kind of secret, I was uneasy. There was, I believe, a new kind of questioning in his eyes. Before, he just wanted me to talk, to tell him what I wanted to tell, but now he wanted more. There was a more complicated light in his eyes, but we tried to act as if nothing had changed. On those drives, we never mentioned the four of us being together. We tried to talk as before, but for me it wasn't working, so I hadn't been to church for several weeks when Mr. Maclean died on that Monday morning.

I drove that day to the same place Russell and I always drove; I parked in the lane, but this time I got out and walked up to the house. I was thinking about Mr. Maclean, about a photograph I had seen of him as a young man. His bearing, his stiff collar and dark suit, his neck and mouth and forehead were severe, but his eyes contradicted all that. He, in that photograph, seemed to be laughing at himself, at his own ambition, at his own serious dream for himself. I was walking in the tall grass beside the house mourning the young Mr. Maclean who also had died that day. I looked in the windows of the lovely old house, at the layers of curling wallpaper and plaster fragments on the worn linoleum. It must have been a graceful house in its day, but it was a terrible mess now, and I could not imagine, as Russell must have been able to, Loretta and him living there. I went up onto the back porch and looked in at the kitchen and then noticed a new scraped arc on the wood porch floor where the sagging screen door had been opened and shut. I pushed the inside door open and then walked around the four downstairs rooms full of litter and light. Upstairs, there were three bedrooms – one on each side of the hallway and a big one at the east end of the house. That big bedroom was as wide as the house was wide, and on three sides were long widows almost to the floor. The lights from the east and north and south seemed to converge and conflict there, and sharp shards of light, reflecting from pieces of a broken mirror on the floor, wavered on the walls. I stood in an east window and looked out over the rolling fields. The room felt like the prow of a ship heading out across these fields on a great journey. Below me in the lane was my car parked where the cabbage man always parked his car. As I turned to go, I noticed below a window sill a neat stack of empty McDonald's coffee cups. This is where the cabbage man came to dream his dream.

That night I almost told Jack the real story of the cabbage man and me, but I didn't.

The next Sunday, I went to church, but he wasn't there. I

sat through the whole Mass, but Russell never came. I went home.

Around noon, Loretta called. "Have either of you seen Russell?"

"No, but don't worry," was about all Jack said.

All afternoon I watched football with Jack. I got a sick feeling and went to lie down.

At five Loretta called again. "I'm worried; this isn't like him." I said, "Loretta, let's go for a drive."

I drove Loretta out to the farm and on the way I told her the whole story. I told her there was nothing between us, just talk, and she looked at me and said, "I know that. I'm not mad at you; I'm mad about that goddamned farm scheme. I thought he had given all that up." She was furious at him, something I'd never imagined, and I got an idea of what it must be like in their house sometimes. I drove fast, trying not to think of what I was beginning to be afraid of.

When we got to the farm, his car was in the lane. We walked to the house through air that seemed as thick to me as water. I couldn't get a whole breath. I took Loretta around back. We pushed open the back door and Loretta was calling, "Russell? Russell?" I went up the stairs, I was so heavy, and she followed me, still calling him. I went to that front bedroom and he was there. I stood in the doorway thinking, if I never let her in the room, she'll never have to see or know. He was lying on his side on the floor, below that east window. He was wearing his blue windbreaker. There were pill bottles beside him, a note. He was dead.

Loretta pushed past me, and standing over him, she screamed and screamed and screamed.

Then she turned to me. I was still in the doorway. She screamed at me: "If you could know this much," and her gesture took in the house and the farm, "why couldn't you know the rest? Why? Why?"

Centripetal forces had been spinning Jack and me apart for years, but the death of Russell Bourget made us slip out of reach of each other, no matter what we willed. We didn't see Loretta anymore. After Russell died, my voice changed; I couldn't just talk, I seemed to shriek. I began to work nights. We were almost never in the house at the same time or, if we were, the other was asleep. I began to work for May.

A few months later, a few months ago, during a long fight one weekend, when both of us were worn down to something like our old voices, Jack turned, on his way out the door for more beer, and just asked, "Janet, what is it that I've done that makes you talk to me like this?"

I laughed and said, "Jack, you don't get it? It's what *I've* done that makes me talk this way."

Jack came back in and sat down on the edge of the couch with his coat still on. "What *you've* done? Why? Tell me the worst thing you've ever done to me."

"The worst, Jack? The very worst?"

Jack was so pale, and, more than anything, he wanted to be out of this room, but he nodded yes.

After a few minutes, I said it.

"I didn't sleep with Russell Bourget. I didn't tell him I loved him."

And then I had to try to explain, but Jack never did understand.

CHAPTER 11

May's Daughter's House

I was coming closer to some yes or no. Both were becoming more familiar to me. I stood beside the Mississippi River with the length of my back against a walnut tree, so my back bent as the tree bent as the wind blew from the west. The sky sent yes and no through the tree to my spine. I stared across the glare of river into tomorrow, the wind, the source of yes, the source of no. I could settle down to live in either country. Soon the time *before* would be over and I would cross a border without noticing it. I would be on the other side where I would know without seeming to have begun to know that *this* was what I was coming to all along.

A breeze at first, then a hot wind straight out of the west. The message arrived first in the raggedy crown of the walnut tree, then arrived at my hair and, then the plantains, their buglike flowers, bumped my sandals in the stiff wind. May was asleep in the sun on the slope of the lawn. The breeze had billowed her pink dress around her thighs and waist, so I weighted her skirt down with rocks from beside the river. She looked like a pink and silver flower bed bordered by rocks.

The smell of the silt in the wind made me think of the summer three years ago when Jack and I drove west to some job interviews and the Pacific Ocean. The driving was so hot, it was like a dream. I don't think either of us said much all the way west, except, "There's a place," or "I'll drive, honey." We just thought about cold drinks and getting there. I remember trying to remember all I'd heard about the ocean. Neither of us had ever been to the ocean.

Jack loved it at once. It was "bracing," he said, and "beautiful," and, from a distance and from the cliffs above, it *was* beautiful and familiar, not strange. What was strange to me was the smell of it. I'd heard "fresh as the sea breeze" and the "bracing salt air" which led me to expect something entirely different. I think I was expecting a multiplication of the smell of rain or of water standing in fields. I expected to like the smell of it, but actually I was shocked, scared even, and, mostly, embarrassed. The smell of it was so personal to be so public. In a way it was like going to the zoo; you think that you're going to go and simply stand outside and look in at an animal, but when you get there you're surrounded by the wild smell of its life. Instead of just coming closer to the animal you've imagined, you're surrounded by it, you're inside of it, and, as you breathe and look, it gets inside of you. Your dream-come-true becomes a joke on you.

Jack and I climbed down one of those cliffs and stood on the sand looking almost *up* at the ocean swelling and falling on the rocks; the waves were so much bigger than the waves I'd imagined. They made me feel like a light-weight, silly, short-lived thing. Yet when I looked down at the sand as we walked on the beach and I saw all the tiny creatures skittering between here and there, and when I saw the million air holes of little animals breathing beneath that sand, and when I saw them numberless in colonies even in small pools, I felt like a giant helplessly causing wreckage with both feet. Jack was pulling me along down the beach behind him and I didn't know if I was coming or going.

And then I saw it all another way. I saw that seeing into the pools and seeing the creatures that clung to the rocks was like seeing alive all the things that a good woman tries to keep her mind off of. All those creatures seemed like just *parts* to me, and private parts at that: Seaweed seemed like the hair of women, shiny tongues poked from bivalves, and holes in the ground made little wet sounds.

The smell of the ocean and the wet whispering and the booming water were hard for a middle-aged midwestern woman to understand. I was curious about the people who lived there year in and year out so close to all that. They must think of as normal things I try not to think about any more; they must talk about things I can't say.

I realized that I was making this trip to Illinois to learn what to say or what to do about who I was — with and without May and Jack and Carl and Russell Bourget. And my father and my mother and sister and a half-sister I've only seen twice. Mr. Maclean and Joyce and Karen and Pat. I was trying to sort — with my skin and my eyes and my breathing and my remembering — what to keep, how far out to draw a line of . . . what? Sisterhood? Eminent domain? Marriage? Duty? I don't yet know the terms for inside and outside.

My back was against that walnut tree, that home base that bent me with it. I used to lean my forehead on trees and count to a hundred, then ransack the farm in the dark looking for Jack and Carl and Joyce. I couldn't wait to get it over with — being *it*, being alone, being watched by them from secret places, being scared to death when they jumped out at me.

Standing with my back against that tree, I saw the hard words to come and I saw the box elder tree in the Hawn's front yard, a tree cut down now for thirty years. Words seem to come from the bark I ripped from that tree. The words are on the bark facing the rotten heart of the tree. Box-elder bark is a good thing to get in your hands when you are a kid: There's the rough out-side bark that makes you remember your own skin for a change, and the satisfying ripping sound when you pull the bark off; on the dusty, smooth, concave side are the words, the tracks, the decorations, the lifelines, the tunnels of the bugs that make sawdust out of wet pink wood. The white prehistoric bugs run from the light, from Hawns' fingers like snouts of anteaters. Brothers and sisters, hold the bark here by the end of it. Feel it's rotten, about to break. A flag for a few minutes marched out in front of you, upright, rotten. Then it breaks in your hand down here and a little is in your hand, the rest is in the grass. One good kick, move on.

In the glare of noon May and I took up so little space; the cir-cles of our existences were small ones. We cast no shadows. Breath was hard to draw from out of the strong, hot wind.

May stirred and then sat up. She pushed the rocks away, laughing. When I gave her a hand to help her up, I saw that she was sweating like a baby after a nap. As we walked to the car, I kept my arm around her waist. I resolved to pull myself to-gether. I was a nurse doing her job.

May's daughter's house turned out to be a big green Victorian one on an old tree-lined street. I looked at the house as we sat in the car for a minute. I brushed May's hair and mine and washed our faces with a washcloth I'd brought along. From the street, this seemed like just what I had hoped for May – space and cool

silence and big trees and a lawn. I felt like a foster parent re-
turning a child to her biological mother.

I wanted to see the daughter first. I told May to wait in the
car. When I was halfway up the brick walk, the screen door
opened with a bang against the side of the house and a compact,
plump, dark-haired woman bustled out. Even from where I
stood on the walk, I could hear her navy nylon dress swish on
her stiff slip and her slip rasp on her girdle. The nylons on her
thighs and calves sang. I was cheered up instantly by this lady.
Her name was Ina Weaver.

"Why, you're right on time! On the dot! After lunch — one
o'clock!" She was almost to me and I was about to be hugged.
"Janet Hawn, you know, people are always late these days, *always, always* late. And here you are! Where is she?" Ina was
looking over my shoulder at May in the car. She whispered
loudly in my ear. "How is she? Is she still out of it? Has she
caused you trouble?"

Ina didn't wait for an answer. She accompanied herself down
the walk and, opening the car door, stood behind it, waiting for
May to get out. May just sat there looking ahead, waiting. It
took more than that to get her to move. "Mother? Mother, do
you know me? It's Ina, Momma." Ina was talking a little too
loud to May, but there was real feeling in her voice. Ina would
get the hang of it pretty soon.

"Stand beside her," I said, "and lift her legs out of the car.
then put your arm around her shoulders and aim her this way."
I watched Ina do what I suggested and watched Ina wait
patiently beside May until May either realized what Ina wanted
or else just decided to get out of the car. Some of the longest moments I have ever spent in my life have been while I waited for
old people to get out of cars. I found myself giggling. Ina, with
her back to me, resting on one leg then the other, was giggling
too.

As May and Ina walked up the narrow brick walk arm in arm
– one foot of each in the grass – I saw something so new come
toward me. What is it, I wondered; it makes me feel happy. It
was not *remembering* or *imagining*. It was a time or air or light
that blessed this procession of two women, mother and daughter, up the walk under these old trees. I waited on the porch
with the screen door open. I had never heard such lovely sounds
as the murmuring of the daughter to the mother, the delicate
steps of their shoes' soles on the brick walk, the frictions of undergarments one upon the other, and, above all that, the sound
of the summer rummaging through the tops of the trees and, beside me, sifting through the screen.

Oddly happy with everything, I followed them into the cool
dark house and shut the screen behind me.

Ina's house smelled new, like sawdust. The entryway, an air-
lock, was raw wood and unpainted sheetrock. Ina began explain-
ing to me what she was having done. "You people up north must
run across this sort of thing every day, but even though we must
have about a month or six weeks less of winter down here than
you do up there . . . " (for a moment I forgot I lived in Wisconsin, wondered why she would think of Half Moon as being either up or more severe) ". . . I can't stand it. I just *can't*, and
every time I came in the front door, I took it *personally* that the
hall would just fill up with winter, so I had them come and put
this in. It's still got to be painted and the woodwork waxed or
oiled or something, I don't know what. You know, it depends on
who you talk to, which hardware store you're in, whether wax
or oil or urethane or paint or stain is just the ticket. Have you
ever had to deal with those guys? Are you married? Yes? Good,
then you can get *him* to deal with these simpletons for you. And
I mean simple, too. These bastards, excuse me, these *idiots,* all
have one answer, all have it narrowed down to one choice and
that's it. If you go into a hardware store – a woman alone, like

me – and you say to one of these all-the-goddamned-answers types 'I want this or I want that,' they say – if they haven't got it or if they, for god knows what reason, don't want to sell it to you – they'll say to you every goddamned time, believe me, Janet, either 'They don't make those any more' or *Lady, that's not what you want.* ' "

We were all three standing in Ina's beautiful Victorian front hall. I was trying to both listen and look. Ina had May and me each by an elbow – shaking mine a bit for emphasis.

" *'Lady, that's not what you want'?* Can you believe that? Who the *hell*," and she gave my elbow a good shake, "do they think I am? Do they think I'm *ignorant?* Do they think I can't *read?* Do they think I don't have *eyes* in my *head?*" Ina stopped to get her breath; her voice had gone about as high as it could. She looked at me and then at May and then she looked embarrassed and let go of us and stepped away from us both. "Oh, I'm *so* sorry? I don't know what came over me. I was just carried away by thinking about incident number 438 this morning, I guess. I should just let you go out and come in again. I should start over."

Ina walked a little circle in the hall composing herself. She straightened her hair and smoothed her face with both hands, and then she smoothed her dress over her hips and took a deep breath. I figured she was about fifty-five. I *liked* her.

"If Momma," and Ina grinned and nodded toward May who was looking up the stairway, "had all her marbles, she would whale my behind for acting like that to my guests. Come on in and sit down and I'll see if I can find my hired teen-ager to bring your stuff in out of the car. You are spending at least the night, aren't you, Janet? Good. You don't mind if I call you 'Janet,' do you? I'm practically old enough to be your mother," by then she was at the back of the house shouting, "so I guess that gives me certain prerogatives."

Ina had sat us both down in a rose and green parlor, a room where the light was subdued by lace panels and filtered through ferns on cast-iron fern stands in the bay window. May sat beside me on the hard, old sofa, fingering the cut-velvet roses on the seat. I could hear Ina in the back yard and then in the cellar calling "Craig! Craig!" She must have found him because I could hear her chewing somebody out and then, while she was rattling glasses and ice in the kitchen, I could hear the doors of my car open and shut and then a heavy, reluctant step on the stairs.

Ina was talking to us before she left the kitchen and the sound of her voice was defining for me the size of her kitchen and hall. "Here's what we'll do." She came in carrying a tray with three glasses of iced tea, and she put it down on a little tea table in front of us. "First we'll wet our whistles and catch our breaths. The old girl," and she nodded toward the silent May, "brought me up *right*. And then I'll, as they say in the movies, 'show you to your rooms' and let you 'freshen up.' Honey," she said, leaning toward me and laying a hand on my knee, "when you're a lady alone and you buy yourself a house like this at the age of fifty, you've got to *live up to it*. People *expect* it, and besides, why else bother." Ina thought this was hilarious, and so did I. She and I both laughed, hand in hand, until we had to take out handkerchiefs and wipe our eyes.

We had our tea and then Ina took us upstairs to our rooms. Ina apologized because mine wasn't finished, but I loved it that way – just a bed and a bureau and the smell of raw wood and the raw light barreling through the windows.

May's room was a room made for May. It was so beautiful, it brought tears to my eyes. I wished I could have done this for May. I was a little jealous.

It was serene and graceful – green and white ivy-patterned wallpaper, dark woodwork, "Priscilla" sheer curtains filtering the southwestern sun. There was a heavy, old bedroom suite, not a good one, walnut veneer from the thirties, it looked like. The heavy arches of the headboard and bureau and the dressing table seemed almost ecclesiastical in their somberness. This seemed a temple to an earlier life. There was a chaste white chenille bedspread on the bed, and under a window, a green-and-white-striped sofa. The dressing table and the walls were covered with photographs in old frames.

May and I both stood in the doorway – I was looking in; May was just looking. Ina gave us both little pushes and I went to look at the photographs on the wall. They were what I hoped they'd be – photographs of May when she was younger. I realized then that in May's house there had not been a single photograph of any earlier time. Here, I was in a museum for May, a museum *of* May and I knew that everything was here for a reason; I wanted to know each reason. I walked around the room looking at the pictures on the wall. There was May, a young girl of about twenty squinting into the light, standing in a yard with her arms around two girl friends. Her hair was blond and her part deep and her figure slim and graceful. There was May as a bride. This time what I saw was round and fair cheeks, a white satin dress without ornament except the volumes of veil, and the man standing next to her a jolly sort who'd never had a doubt in his life; big shoulders, big face, kind eyes, vast chin. There was a tinted studio portrait of a strawberry-blond, plump woman, with a dark-haired little girl – clearly the older daughter, not Ina. "What's her name?" I asked. "Francine," she said and sighed. "She was a *great* little girl, but now she's a dependent, miserable shrew in Cleveland. I miss her." There was May again; I guess it was May; the context told me it was May, but this woman was a friendly laughing woman with no eyebrows and a sundress, her tanned, bare arms tight around her plump, pale daughters. Her mouth was reshaped by red lipstick; her whole face seemed redrawn. Then there she was with her husband who was now a little more solemn, but she was thin and severe with her hair drawn straight back and her eyebrows dark arches, her mouth pale. I looked at Ina and started to speak.

"I know," she said. "She never looked like the same person. Everybody notices that, and that was the thing about Mother. It was true in real life too. One time, Francine came home from camp when she was eight years old, they told this one over and over, and she didn't recognize for a few minutes her own mother."

We looked at May. She had sat down in a rocker by the window, in the sun. She was looking out the window and a small breeze was ruffling her hair. She reminded me of old Mr. Maclean's cat, now my cat, Tom. She looked comfortable here. Was Jack remembering to feed Tom? Of course he was. Was Jack remembering to eat supper? I hoped so.

"You know, Janet," Ina was leaning on the doorframe and looking at her mother. She looked a little tired. "I wish I knew whether doing this was kindness on my part or cruelty. I mean fixing this room like this, putting in it all the things that Mother hated and discarded over the years as being old-fashioned or out-of-style or god knows why, unacceptable. She hated this furniture, couldn't wait till she could afford better stuff, gave it to Francine as soon as Francine moved out of the house. All these photographs, the doilies, the curtains – all this was hers or was like what she had. I've told myself alternate stories. 'I'm recreating the past for a woman who doesn't have one anymore.' 'I'm forcing a woman to be the way we always wanted her to be, and to stay with the things she hated.' You know she's a much nicer person now than she ever was when she knew what was what. I like her now. I couldn't live with her before. It's a terrible thing to say, but each time I'd go visit Mother in Green Bay and each time I saw her more and more out of it and more and more serene like this and dignified, the better I liked it." Ina pushed herself with her hands that were behind her away from the doorframe. "But who could fault me, right?" She laughed and went to May. "A daughter taking in her senile old mother – the daughter with a big house and nobody else? What else could she do but this – fix a nice room for her pretty old mother? Who could fault me, right?"

Ina and I unpacked May's few things and put them into the clean and sweet-smelling closet and drawers. It was all so nice. Who could fault her? May sat there happy like a cat in the sun. Ina and I went downstairs.

Ina said she would show me all over her house, but first she excused herself and went in her bedroom and changed her clothes. She must have taken off all her structural undergarments because in that light blue sweat suit she put on she looked twenty pounds heavier and she didn't make any noise when she walked. She was shorter too, in her Nikes.

We went back upstairs and checked on May periodically, but Ina showed me every room in her house and I loved it. She showed me the new furnace and the new water heater, poked and patted them like they were expensive pets she kept in the basement. She showed me her table saw and showed me that she could rip a board on it. I was suitably impressed. She took me upstairs and we went through the kitchen, cupboard by cupboard, drawer by drawer. She showed me the kind of hardware she'd finally settled on for the doors and showed me her first choice which they wouldn't take back at the goddamned lumber yard because it was a special order, the bastards. In the dining room she stroked the smooth papered walls and told me the stories of how many kinds of jerks she had hired before she finally got somebody who would take the old paper off right.

Craig appeared now and then in the yard. I got glimpses of "His Sullenness" – as Ina called him – as he mowed the yard looking as if each step pained him. He looked permanently embarrassed and reluctant. He was pushing an old-fashioned reel mower. Ina noticed me notice the mower, as she was showing me where the library shelves would go in. "Isn't that posture of his hysterical? I don't suppose I should, but I love seeing the ridiculousness of his every move. Craig! He is mortified that he has to mow the yard with an old-fashioned mower like that. He wants me to let him bring over his dad's riding mower, but I will not have one of those things on the place, so he remains scared that one of his high-school friends will see him and I guess impugn his manhood. Poor Craig. Now, come on, I want to show you what I'm doing with the upstairs bathroom." And she took me upstairs into a bright white-tiled room with big, old footed fixtures, and told me the story of the Portuguese tile man and the electrician.

There had been scheduling problems, she said, and each wanted to work last because he was sure the other would screw up his work and she couldn't get either one to come. This went on for months. Finally she called them both one day and said the same thing to each of them. "Now why don't you come finish the job? The other will have finished, and then I'll have a nice lunch for two when you're done." They both fell for it. They both came over the next morning, one at eight, the other at eight-thirty, and when Ina let them in the house she made sure that she walked them by the beautifully set table for two with flowers and wine glasses. They both went upstairs with smiles on their faces, until the Portuguese tile man, the second one to come, saw the electrician at work in the bathroom and they both realized they'd been had. She said they both finished their jobs that day, but the cursing and swearing, half of it in Portuguese, left a film of blue on the tiles. When they were finished, Ina said she forced them to sit at the table together and eat the elegant meal together while she inspected the job and wrote them their checks. I sat on the edge of the tub while she told me this story.

I could almost smell those men – their cursing and their sweat – in this room. Ina patted her pipes and stroked her tiles. This whole house was alive for her; it was an unruly, adolescent, male beast she was taming; she knew its every fault and its every virtue; she knew its limits, but she knew, more than anyone, its possibilities; it was a world she was wrenching for herself from out of the world of men.

We checked on May. She was lying on the bed, asleep. We crept back out silent and backwards, like two new parents away from the crib of the bad kid.

Ina said she was going to lie down for a few minutes before she started supper, but I was to make myself right at home. I said I would use the phone if she didn't mind. She took me in to the unfinished library and shut the door behind her when she left.

I sat down on a pile of walnut shelving. Where did this woman get all her money, I wondered. Obviously there was a lot of it.

The house and the yard and the street were silent around me, though there was some racket from sparrows in the bushes in front of the house and in the gutters. A block or so away I could hear a bell clanging at a railroad crossing and, as I concentrated, I could hear or feel the rumble of the freight through this drowsy town. Finally I picked up the phone and punched in the little song that was our phone number. It rang and rang. Jack was out. I imagined the sound of the phone poking little stabs like light into the ears of the cat, Tom, the only receiver there. He wouldn't deign to open his eyes, only twitch his ears in annoyance as the phone woke him out of sleep, then go back to sleep in the sun when I hung up. Jack. Where are you?

I went upstairs and turned back the spread. I shut the door and locked it. I took off all my clothes and went immediately to sleep in the sun between Ina Weaver's good sheets.

When I woke up, it felt late. I dressed quickly and checked on May. She wasn't in her room. There were voices, I thought, coming from the kitchen. Voices? I ran downstairs, and down the hall, and stood in the kitchen doorway.

May was standing in the back door looking in. Ina was standing at the sink, talking. "I thought I heard voices... "

Ina, with her hands in the sink, looked at me, smiling, but then, seeing the expression on my face, she became serious. "No, honey, she didn't say anything. It was just me talking. It was just me going on and on to her. She never was this good of a listener before." Ina laughed and dried her hands.

Now Ina had on a housedress, a green and white cotton housedress with a white pique collar, and her white sandals were old-lady sandals. Her hair was rolled up tighter. She looked rested and rosy. "I made you a gin and tonic. How does that sound? I took a chance; you might be a teetotaler, but if that was the case I could always drink it myself." Ina handed me a drink with almost melted ice, but with fresh mint in it and lime.

"Can I help you do something?" I offered.

"No, you just set still. It's harder for me to figure out what needs doing and then say it, than it is for me to do it myself. And I'm just making us a light supper. But if you wanted to peel this cucumber, I wouldn't mind." She handed me a knife and cucumber on a cutting board, and pulled out a chair at the kitchen table for me. I sat down, and it felt good to be doing something with my hands.

Ina rummaged around in the refrigerator for something, and then, not finding it, she turned to me. "Does Mom *ever* talk?"

"No, she hasn't for a year or so." Ina surprised me, because her eyes filled with tears. I told her about the few things May used to say to me. A sentence here or there criticizing what I was wearing or what I cooked. Now and then a complaint about being old. I told Ina about the time May had become furious and cursed at two people, Fritz and Judy, and threw coffee cups. "Who were Fritz and Judy?" I realized that I assumed that they were dead, perhaps because now May seemed to have erased them from her memory and I realized how awful it was for Ina that in a way her past, too, had disappeared, if her own mother no longer remembered the moment of her birth, if no one but Ina herself remembered Ina the little girl.

"I never heard of any Fritz or Judy. They're maybe friends of Mom's and Dad's, people I don't know."

Then I told Ina about May at night, about how she wouldn't stay in the house, about the walks she would take through the parks and the suburbs and I told Ina about the empty, falling-down house that she used to go and stare into. "What was that house to her? Do you know?"

Ina had stopped bustling around her kitchen and sat down opposite me at the table. She had me tell her several times where the house was and what it looked like. "Why do you think she went there?" I asked. Ina reached across the table and gripped my hand, squeezing it around the paring knife handle, started to speak, then got up and walked over to May.

"Mom," Ina held May by her upper arms and shook her a little, gently. Ina was shorter than May, but here in Ina's kitchen, though she was silent and mysterious, May played a bit part. "Mom. May. Katherine May Moore. Mother." May did not respond. She was so much like a cat. You could talk to her, and there was a semblance of alertness, yet there were no words that came back to you and nothing that you said or did seemed to have a corresponding reaction in her. You could aim her toward nothing with your hands or your voice.

There was no response from May. Ina came back and sat down at the table with me, defeated. Then she got up and began to fix us each another gin and tonic. "I've never seen that house," she said without looking at me or May. "But I know what that house must be. I've gotten pieces of the story from Francine and pieces from a friend of my mom's, Darcy, who I used to go visit in the nursing home, when I'd go up and see mom in Green Bay. Darcy died about five years ago."

"Wait," I said, "Ina, do you think we should talk like this in front of her, as if she can't hear?"

Ina looked at May and then at me. "Well, I don't know." This hadn't occurred to her. She sliced a lime and squeezed it into our glasses while she thought about it. "I think it's OK," she said. Then with more conviction, "I think it's fine. What if she *did* understand and react in some way to even everything we say? The worst that could happen, I think, is that she would know that we are interested in her, we want to remember her, we want to know about her. I really believe," Ina said now with vehemence, gesturing with lime in her hand spreading the smell of the lime all over the kitchen, "that *interest,* that *curiosity* is the sincerest expression of love." Again there were tears in her eyes. "I was married to a man for years who, if he had once eavesdropped on a phone conversation, or opened my mail, or asked me what it was like to do what I did, or if I had the remotest inkling from a word or a gift that he tried to imagine what my life was like while he was not in the room, I wouldn't have divorced him and tried to take him for every red cent he was worth." She laughed and wiped her eyes. "Luckily," and her gesture took in the house, "he was worth a lot. On paper." Ina sniffed, and wiped her eyes on her sleeves. "So, no, I think it's fine to talk about her and wonder about her in front of her. We love her and she's interesting. If she was just a dull old broad we didn't care about, we wouldn't bother."

May had been all this time standing beside the refrigerator at the screen door half turned toward the leafy back yard. I got up and took a kitchen chair to her and got her to sit down in it. She looked like a woman at a bus stop shelter who knows the bus will be a long time coming, but really doesn't mind the wait.

Ina handed me my fresh gin and tonic, then was silent while she rubbed a roasting chicken all over with butter and upended it, stuffing in some onion and herbs. When she leaned over the oven, adjusting the chicken's legs, tying them tighter, I recognized in her sturdy posture that of every woman I had ever known and that of myself. I saw myself as one in a long line of women who wrench out of a foreign and hostile world, the stuff to make meals and days out of. For the first time, I longed for the daughter Jack and I hadn't had the time or money or nerve or place to have.

Ina wiped her buttery hands on her apron and sat down at the table with some lettuce and tomatoes and onions. "My mother is and was an interesting woman, but of course the last thing you want when you're a child is an interesting mother. She behaved more outrageously than almost anybody I've ever heard of in that era, so much so that Francine, the year she was fourteen, refused to go to school in our town, because she was teased so unmercifully about May. I can still hear it too: 'Mother *may* I? No, but May may!' But I was a little girl, about seven, that year, 1937, and Francine was fourteen and *sensitive*. Lord, was she sensitive, but that's another story. As a girl I just knew that my mother was disgraced, and I never really knew until later what had gone on.

"My father was a busy man. He was even then beginning to convert the factory to making gear systems for guns; previously it had been farm machinery – your classic plows into swords. So Dad was busy and Mother often took us two girls on the train down to Chicago to see her mother; then more and more frequently she would go by herself and she would get someone to stay with us girls." Ina paused and took a deep breath. "What happened is that she met a man on the train, which is bad enough in itself, but this was a man, it's hard to believe this could happen in 1937, who was a black man, a Negro, and, if it can be any worse in the public's opinion, he was a porter on the train." Ina looked at me and shook her head and took several deep breaths. Then she went on. "The only thing this man wasn't was married, though that didn't seem to make much difference to anybody, because of course everyone found out. Everyone. She was seen with him as bold as life on State Street in Chicago. She didn't go to her mother's; she stayed with this man in a *hotel*, in the black district, and men in Dad's factory, as well as others told him about it. But they didn't really have to because Mom didn't seem to care whether anyone knew or not. She even began to stay with this man in his house in *Green Bay*. And that, I'm afraid, is the house she walked you to: John Ash's house. My mother came home one day at suppertime, her friend Darcy and also Francine later told me; she had said she was going to Chicago that morning to see her mother. She came in the door and, before she even got to the dining room where my father was eating, being served by the woman who came in to help, she said in a cheerful voice clear as a bell, "Albert, I'm leaving you. I came to get my things. I'm going to live with a man named John Ash who loves me." And she went upstairs. My father, I hear, finished his supper and didn't say a word. Mother did move out and I don't know why I don't remember any of this. I often wonder where I was, what sort of blind child I was, but I really don't remember anything but a strong feeling that disaster surrounded us and I didn't know from which direction it would finally come to do us in. I just remember fear as something that I inhaled with each breath.

"Very gradually, this feeling left the house, because after a short time – I heard two days, and I heard two weeks – my father went and got her and brought her back. John Ash was – incredibly – not lynched or even beat up, but he lost his job on the railroad, apparently before my father went for my mother. It may be that he had even left town before Father went to that house and packed my mother's things and brought her back to our house. Somehow I think that's the way it was; my father was a strong-willed man, but not a combative one. That would have been his style – to quietly get rid of the man, and then, without a word, bring her back."

We both looked at May who was still waiting for that bus. "And that, as far as I know, is the end of the story. Our household got over it all as you get over a serious disease. After about a year we seemed to have our strength back – though not our social status – and everything was fairly normal. Mother never did anything like that again."

Ina and I were silent. We finished cutting the vegetables for the salad, but we were both seeing Katherine May Moore Nickelson, an old lady, standing outside of John Ash's empty house. Ina put the salad in the refrigerator. "I haven't shown you my back yard," she said. "Let's take Mother outside too." And we went outside to look.

CHAPTER 12

Dancing with a Dying Man

What I was trying not to think about was Carl Hawn whom I knew had lived for years alone in the house where he grew up. Shirley left him for good not long after Jack and I left the farm and now the house was falling down around him, the land rented out or lost to the bank. What I was trying not to think about was Jack Hawn sitting at the kitchen table in a condominium that could be anywhere, in a town where we don't know anyone. What I was trying to keep my mind off of was that fork in the road ahead of me. My foot was in that road.

After supper May and Ina and I went for a walk. I saw right away that Ina did not live, as I at first thought she did, in a settled and secure old neighborhood that would always be this way. At the end of her block was a convenience store, a gas station, and on the next block a feed mill whose smell of rotting soybeans was overpowering, she said, when the wind was right "or wrong." Many of these big old houses were at one time rooming houses and now were divided into apartments, but still some were pretty and there were lots of families with children. We had to step around a Big Wheel on almost every block, and little children, who had worn the grass off the yards just like chickens do, came off the porches to stare or smile at us. I liked it here and found myself wondering which of these places Jack and I could live in when we lost the condominium.

Later, while Ina bathed May and got her ready for bed, I tried to call Jack again, but there was no answer. There was no one to call to check on him. What a way to live! We had to get out of there. Without me, Jack had no one there. And I had no one without him. I knew Jack would not kill himself; my worry for him was not that, but that he would somehow permanently embarrass himself from need. From frustration. From getting a look at his own loneliness.

I called the Half Moon Hotel to tell Dad that I would be there tomorrow afternoon, but he was out, too. The girl at the desk said she would give him the message. She said he was probably at the Dairy Queen getting his nightly hot fudge sundae.

Around ten o'clock, Ina and I decided to try to get May to go to bed. We led her to it and pulled back the covers and Ina patted the bed like you do a chair you want a dog to jump up on. May got in the bed just fine, without reluctance, and Ina and I looked at each other in triumph. Now, if we can just get her to stay there. I sat with her while Ina got a basket of buttons and ribbons and sewing odds and ends that she had saved from years and years ago. Maybe it had been May's mother's; Ina wasn't sure. Then, while May sat in bed with a shawl around her shoulders and played with the odds and ends – taking them out and putting them back as she had the basket of things from Fan Butcher and the Ohio Motel – Ina and I sat on the couch under the windows in May's bedroom and waited. After a little bit, Ina started telling me a story about where she'd gotten the green-and-white-striped ticking to cover the couch and about the upholsterer she'd talked into doing the work for sixty dollars, but this time I was only half listening. I was thinking ahead to seeing my father again and to being in Half Moon and I was wondering where I would stay there; I hadn't given it any thought. I was seeing some places in the road near home, a farmhouse with no trees around it in the center of a field; a hedgerow; a house with windows that looked like eyebrows; a graceful crab apple tree in a valley near Sugar River; a rock on a corner fence post by a stop sign; the curve in the road near the elevator at Greene; and then the first view of Half Moon, "The Town on Five Hills," after that curve.

The night air coming in the windows was chilly and smelled like fields. Ina got up and closed them both most of the way, dimmed the light by May's bed, and brought me a sweater and us both an afghan. "Put your feet up," she said, "and put this over your legs." So we both settled in at each end of the sofa with our feet in the middle covered by the same afghan.

It was soothing sitting there in the near-dark while May played with those sewing things, as it is to sit in a room with a man or woman intent on making something. I remember one afternoon in Carl and Shirley's kitchen not long after Jack and I were married. Shirley and I were putting up the last of the tomatoes and we were working quickly without talking, trying to get finished. I remember our hands slipping the skins off the scalded tomatoes and stuffing them in the quart jars and I remember Carl, his chin on his hands there at the table watching our hands. He had work to do – Jack had already gone back out to the field – but Carl sat a long time and just watched us. He seemed so content in the kitchen with Shirley and me canning tomatoes. It was nice, too, having him there, though neither of us said so; his watching gave grace to the small and repeated actions of our hands. I wondered how much contentment like that Carl had had since those days. From the sound of things, according to my father, not very much. As I sat with Ina and watched May's hands, I realized that I was facing east, the farm; I felt that I was on the circumference of the circle that the farm was the center of; from the edge of this circle it was a straight line to the house and to Carl; I was in range of Carl.

After a while I asked Ina, "Do you think it would have been better if May had stayed with John Ash?"

Ina, in a voice more contemplative than her daylight voice, finally answered. "I don't know. I don't think so, really. It didn't make any sense, her and John Ash. Doesn't it have to make sense? I mean, isn't that what marriage, the whole business, is for — to make some small amount of sense of the world? Albert and I made no sense together."

May dumped all the buttons and bows out again on the bed and some of the buttons fell on the floor. Ina and I crawled around retrieving them, then settled down again to wait for May to sleep. "Tell me about your husband, Janet. Is he a good man?"

"Oh yes, he's good, but he is . . . I don't know the word for it." I saw Jack again in my mind's eye, a good, just man sitting at the kitchen table — stalled and without the vision to see, this time, his way out. I saw myself next to him, exasperated with his plight which was somehow no longer mine. I saw myself leave him yesterday, saw the distance widen between us, as it widens between flotsam caught in two different currents of the same river. I saw, as if from a great distance, Jack going under. "There is a phrase for it, though. Jack is a farmer with a farm under a lake." And I found the voice to tell Ina the story my grandfather Orin Check had told us kids over and over about the hired man that Grandpa "Deecy" Hawn had called "the preacher Eldgrim." Deecy was Jack and Carl's grandfather.

I told Ina that one early summer day in the late twenties, Deecy Hawn and Orin Check were sitting on Deecy's back step, getting ready to go back out to work when they saw a tall man walking across Deecy's field. At the end rows the man's strides were wide as he tried every other furrow, then too short and comical when he stepped on the top of each one. "Whoever that man is, he's no farmer," Deecy said to my grandfather. The man came right up to them and introduced himself as Warren Eldgrim, and he said he was looking for work.

"Everybody's looking for work," one of them said, probably Deecy. And the other said that there's plenty of work everywhere you look; there's just no money for doing it. Eldgrim had just acquired some land, but he had no money and no skill in making money and he had no knowledge of farming, so he wanted to work for Deecy Hawn to learn to farm; he had heard that Deecy Hawn was the farmer, who, if there was one dollar to be made in farming, would be the one to make that dollar. He would work for Deecy for a year for room and board, so that he could go back to his land, then farm it himself. It was good river-bottom land, he said, though there wasn't much of it. Eldgrim was a serious man, with white hands, and he was, my grandfather said, a bit "poetical" in his speech.

Eldgrim stayed fourteen years at the Hawns and never went home to Hull because a government dam project put Eldgrim's land at the bottom of Sugar Lake. He never preached around Half Moon, though now and then women with trouble would go and wait in Deecy Hawn's wife's dark parlor, and they'd cry there while she went out to the field to bring back Eldgrim for their solace. The Hawn family got bigger, some said with help from Eldgrim, but other than that, there was no more story to

Eldgrim's life, just silence, endurance, shame. He just worked for Deecy Hawn, then died one spring of an influenza that killed young or old or weak ones. He was a preacher with no church, a bookish man who never read, a farmer with a farm under a lake.

I still remembered the story. Each next part of that story appeared in front of me like the next part of a familiar road. Though I couldn't picture the whole road, at each point where the story turned, I remembered which way it went. "My grandfather had a funny way of telling those stories – a funny formal way with those stories."

"I liked it," Ina said. "I like your grandfather's voice." Ina was looking at me curiously. "What does that tell me about your husband?"

"Not much really, but it tells you where he comes from, and it tells you that Jack is like that farmer with a farm under a lake. Jack is also a man out of context, away from the place where his people are, a man separated all his adult life from doing the work he wanted to do, living the life he wanted to live."

"It's terribly *sad*," said Ina, leaning forward, "and these days – all these damaged men – it's awfully common."

"I know," I said, but I laughed when I said it.

"How could it be funny?" Ina asked, a little indignant.

We both were watching May who was now leaning back on the fat pillows. Her eyes were closed, but her hands were still busy in that basket.

"Oh Jack's situation isn't funny; it's just something I remembered about the Preacher Eldgrim, something I haven't thought about for, I bet, thirty years. We kids who grew up together," I told Ina, "Jack, and Joyce, and Carl and I, had somehow got it in our heads that Eldgrim was the bogey man – a combination fool and fiend – and our worst insult was "*You* are the *bastard grandchild* of the preacher Eldgrim!" It was probably just the name that was funny to us, but we made him into a ghost – the one who preceded us and the one who would come after us. I remember arguments that lasted for hours about which bedroom on the square mile Eldgrim had died in. We found out at some point that he had died in a little hired man's house that had been torn down for years, but, even knowing that, we still liked to choose one of the four of us to pick on for a while and construct evidence that proved conclusively that it was, for example, *Joyce's room* where Eldgrim had died in horrible agony, cursing the Hawns and their progeny."

As I told Ina about Eldgrim, I saw the four of us kids on the back step at the Hawns bickering away an afternoon – the same back step on which our grandfathers sat when they first caught sight of poor Warren Eldgrim, the same back step where Joyce as a little girl sang to the cats, the same step where Carl stood so many years before listening to his wife bathe his children. The step was still there and the house, and Carl was still in the house, though everything else – our house and the people and most of the outbuildings and the fences and the hedges and the ownership of most of the land – was gone.

I stood up. Carl was still there. The house was there and the yard and the back step and the back porch that probably still smelled like cats and the garden and greasy overalls. I was eighty miles away from this place that was not just an idea we had lost, but a real place. While I was in this room with May and Ina, Carl was in one of the rooms of that house. And Carl was real; he was not just an idea of myself I had given up.

I turned to Ina. "I'm going to go back there right now. I know it's rude, but I don't mean to be rude. It's only an hour and a half or so from here." We looked at May. She was lying back on the pillows; her hands were still and her eyes were closed. She might be asleep. "Ina, don't even get off the couch." Disentangling my feet from the afghan, I stood in front of her and held her hands. "You are my friend and I will not let you and May fall out of my life. I'll be back to see you. I intend to keep you for a friend until I'm dead."

"More likely I'll be dead first, but I know what you mean, honey. Now you go do what you have to do. You know where to find me and you know you're welcome any time." She squeezed my hand, and then I kissed May lightly on the cheek, and I left.

All these damaged men — that's the phrase Ina had used. I heard it as I drove and I drove fast. There was no one on the two-lane roads, no car lights ahead of me or behind me, and there were few lights out there on all that flat land, except for the occasional pale green glow of a small town. There were no fences anymore or hedges or rows of cedars to stop the wind or the light or the eye — even in the dark. The land was a low black factory all around me, boiling with the slow green seethe that is a field in summer. There were almost no people left on this prairie that was now square-mile fields, but on the road in the dark at midnight I felt them around me. *All those damaged men.* Men driving alone. Men sitting in bars constructing atmospheres with beer and talk. Men awake alone in kitchens. Men watching movies on TV. Men damaged by war and work and no work and work in the wrong place for the wrong people. Men working for the wrong reasons, to take care of the wrong women. Men — and women, too — out of place, out of time, out of luck, alone.

I thought again of the best woman I had ever heard of. I'd heard about her from other nurses who took care of the aged in their homes. I don't know her name; she was a woman in her fifties, taking care of a frightening man — tall and wild-eyed and mean with what we used to call senility. He would not rest or eat or stop cursing or even sit down when she first went to his home, but she noticed right away that when music was on he seemed more calm and he seemed to move his body to the music. One day she put on a record — I don't know what music — and she asked him to dance with her. And he did. It clearly gave him pleasure and peace; then he could rest. After that the woman danced every day with this apparition, this skeleton in pajamas who scared away the young nurses. She danced with him every day three and four hours at a time until it seemed that he could rest. She danced with this dying man every day until almost the day he died. Whenever I thought of her, she gave me courage.

I drove very fast on the almost empty highway and got to the turnoff to the farm in a little more than an hour. Then I drove slowly on the gravel road and I drove clear around the square-mile section, clear around what had been the Hawns' and the Checks' farms. There is the part of darkness that filled in the room where the preacher Eldgrim died. That is the darkness that the hedge trees used to thrash and windmills used to fan, there is where Jack's and Nelda's arms used to conjure the future, and there is where our house used to be. From that spot on earth we used to spy on the Hawns.

I could feel the house in my chest, an ache as though the corners of the house pressed inside of me. How could it mean so much and yet be gone? How can that which is only inanimate be animated merely by association, by messages sent from the outside, through the senses, through the skin? I want to study the relationship of the surface of the body to the air. I want to know how it is that that which is commonest – the air and the light we walk in – can give up so much to us and yet still be not enough. How do we get so much through the surfaces of our bodies from the turn of the bird in the air, from the breezes and clouds that go on by, from walls and dishes and sheets, from kisses and caresses, from the touch of another's skin on ours? How is it that our surfaces are so permeable, so insubstantial, so alert, so passive, so hungry? How is it that mere colors and mere breezes and mere kisses can go through the skin to the heart?

Though the yard light was not on at Carl's, there were lights in the house. I parked the car where everyone had always parked, and, reaching out in the dark, felt the gate where my hand and arm still knew it was. My feet remembered the walk and the steps and the porch floor. My back remembered to catch the outside door before it slammed. The porch smelled like the same Hawn mingling of animal and vegetable and mineral – this vestibule between animal and human. I was sure of what I knew, and happy. I opened the inside door to the kitchen and called, "Carl?" The house smelled unfamiliar – smoky and male and closed. There was no answer, but I could hear the television on low in the front room. I went on into the kitchen. Two big, pale cats jumped down off the counter and disappeared into the pantry. "Carl?" In the dining room there were men's clothes folded on the table and hanging on the chairs. Carl must live downstairs, in these three rooms; this is where he kept his clothes. I stood in the doorway to the front room and there was Carl, just the way I imagined him to be, only worse. He was lying on the sofa asleep, facing away from me and the television. One arm was over his eyes, his nose was mashed against the back of the sofa and his mouth was open; he was snoring. He looked bad – he was unshaven, his hair long and dull, his skin pale.

I turned off the TV, and left on the little lamp behind the sofa, but Carl didn't wake up. I moved aside a few empty beer cans and ashtrays and sat down on the footlocker that Carl used for a coffee table. For a long time I just sat there and looked at him; I was looking for the young Carl I used to know, for his resemblance to Jack, and both were there. Now Carl looked more like the Jack I married than Jack did; the broad bones of his face made me remember the younger Jack, though the skin under his eyes, too, was thin and revealing. Carl seemed to be revising himself back toward his bones while Jack was putting on weight like it was real estate. Carl slept on, his breathing hard. I moved his arm away from his face and moved his face away from the back of the sofa so his breathing was easier. He still didn't wake up. He was very drunk.

I watched him as he slept, saw him as no one wants to be seen, but as everyone wants to be loved – dirty and coarsened and grey, in the midst of trying on death. I didn't want him to wake up; I didn't know what to say to him. If you don't talk to people, you forget how: I think I said this out loud, but Carl didn't wake up. In my mind I listed all the languages I had once known, but had lost from disuse – the French language and the language of family and friendship, the private local language of childhood, and the sweet language of the body in love.

I lifted Carl's heavy right arm and laid it across my lap. Under the brown skin of his forearm there was movement as there is in any live thing; his arm was reacting, I guess, to me and to a dream and to the spinning of the earth through space. Carl's fingers were relaxed and graceful, though his nails were broken, and when I put my fist under his warm dry palm, his hand closed on mine and held it for a moment in his sleep. When his hand let go again, I touched the back of it and his wrist; then with my thumb and my forefinger, I traced the bones along the outside of his hand and his arm, where the broad hand joins the narrow wrist. No matter what someone says or doesn't say or wants you to know about himself, that branching of long bones and muscle and skin into thumb and fingers says – involuntarily – something true. I think I can read there the balance of delicacy with strength. I remembered Carl's hands on steering wheels and Jack's hands too. The backs of Jack's hands were prideful and vulnerable and eloquent; Carl's hands were more knowing and they caught the air. I loved both of these Hawns.

In his sleep Carl turned toward the back of the sofa, pulled his arm away from my hands and drew his hand under his face. I stood up and from the corner of my cyc saw something shining at me from the dark. Cats' eyes. The two cats had silently settled into the big chair by the window behind me and were watching me watch Carl. Some bank of air had shifted and now the night air came through the open windows – not in little breezes, but pouring in like rivers of cold water. I should have been cold, but then and there I would have been at home in a wide range of climates. I covered Carl with the ratty red blanket I found on the floor beside the sofa, one that the teen-aged Hawn boys used to keep in the trunk of the green Ford.

Then I moved the cats aside and sat down in their big chair where I could see both Carl and the night sky. The cats settled down again on my lap. They didn't care who I was; anyone warm would do.

A lot had been lost – money and land and time and parts of families, but this house and this farm were still *inhabited*. We had almost lost everything, but there was enough here, I thought, to fan to life. There was Carl and the Carl who used to be and the old man Carl who wouldn't give up on the others. I knew that. I knew what Carl was doing here: There was an old farmer he had a vision of; he was determined to grow into that skinny taciturn old man.

As I sat watching, the room began to be crowded, not with ghosts, but with presences from the past and future – guardians. The young, smart Jack and the wise man he could become. Ghostly Joyce, the three Carls. I was there, too, at sixty – bossier, quicker, fatter – a little like Nelda and like Ina and my own mother. And beyond was one who scared me – a paling eighty-year-old woman who, like May, had lost her words which, as I thought about it, were all that connected the spirit to the body, our earth to all that sky. And, oddly, watching over us all was the girl Janet at twenty who knew things then that she never spoke about even to herself, who knew things about the body and the earth and the air that all of us had forgotten. I saw that at forty I had been trying to simplify as Jack had always

simplified for us: Who and how did I love twenty years ago? Was
I wrong to marry Jack? Who do I love more? But all of us Janets
together know that those questions cannot really be answered,
only acknowledged. We all should have acknowledged, perhaps
even spoken of, love and want and doubt and fear.

I sat there a long time and when the night was deepest and
coldest and most quiet, I knew that I was really here and I was
reinhabited by all my other selves and my voice. I pushed the
cats off my lap and went into the kitchen. I took the phone into
the pantry the way Jack used to when he was a teen-ager and
talked on the phone to me for hours. I shut the door and sat
down on the floor and called Jack.

I could hear that he answered before he was awake and before
he controlled the fear in his voice. "Oh, Jan, where are you? Are
you OK, honey? Is it an accident?"

"No, Jack, I'm fine. There's nothing wrong."

"Oh, thank God. Thank God." Jack was sitting up in bed now
and I could hear him switch on the light and try to slow down
his breathing. I knew that he was looking right at our clock
when he asked me, "What the hell time is it? Where are you?
What's going on?"

"I just called to hear your voice, Jack. To hear what's in it.
You *do* miss me, don't you. I could hear it."

"Of course I do. Where are you now? At the old lady's daughter's?" Now I could hear Jack's situation crowding into his voice,
pinching it. He was remembering that he had no work and no
real place, that I was, at best, remote from him and so was his
family.

"Jack, I'm at your place. The Hawn place. Carl's."

There was a long silence. I listened to Jack's breathing while
he tried to figure the possibilities and what to say. He decided he
needed more information. "Who else is there?" he asked me.

"Just Carl."

"What is going on, Janet?" He didn't know, so this time he just *asked* me. Twenty years ago he just assumed he knew what it was and twenty years ago the last thing he wanted was to hear me talk about it. And twenty years ago, talk was the last thing I could do.

Then I told him what had happened: that I had been sitting there talking to Ina Weaver and all of a sudden I had to be here at the farm, I had to see Carl and this place. I came here and found him drunk and asleep, and I sat and thought about some things for awhile.

"What am I supposed to think about this? Or do? I don't know what's going on in your head right now."

"You never did, Jack, but that's not just your fault. I'll just tell you." And I did. I told him I wasn't coming back there; I was staying here in Illinois. I told him that he should come here too. "Believe me, Jack, you're needed here. There's work to do here."

"There may be work to do, but there's no money in the work. Be realistic, Janet. Talk sense."

"We can figure out something. We can live here. We need to be here, to start over."

In Jack's voice I could hear the undercurrent of excitement that was beginning to sweep him away, that he wanted to be swept away by, but I could also hear his surface sense, the veneer of bitter experience in his words. "Janet, I have an interview in Sturgeon Bay the day after tomorrow. It's a good job. I have a good shot at this one. I can't just walk out like this and you can't either – walk out on me."

"We're nowhere there. We need to be here. Remember how visible the future was when we were here? Remember the garden I was going to make you with only blue flowers in it? Remember the orchards we would have and . . . "

"For Christ *sake,* you *have* to be realistic, just a little. You know and I know, though I will not mention any names, that others have dreamed that dream and killed themselves doing it. And Carl doesn't seem to be doing too good there with that idea. You haven't even *talked* to him about this."

Then I listed for him all the things that needed doing, just the things that I could see. I knew Jack. "Listen," I said, "most of the storm windows aren't even off yet and the fence is falling down; the porch needs new screens; there's just piles of things all over the downstairs here and outside there's a big branch half fallen off one of the maples, it landed on the porch, and sparrows are nesting in the eaves. Besides, there's not a thing to eat in this pantry and it's full of mouse droppings, even with two cats in the house."

After a moment and very slowly he said, "You and I and Carl? Carl?"

"Not here, Jack, in this house. Not the three of us. I was coming to that. You and Carl here and me in town at the hotel or someplace. I want to live by myself again for a while. But I want to work on this place with you and Carl. I want to start over."

For a long time he didn't say anything, but after a while I could hear that his breathing was beginning to churn itself into sobs, deep and hard. I just talked and talked to him, nonsense really, but words of love. I called him by all my old love names for him and told him what to bring and to be sure and not forget the cat and how the cat would like these two cats maybe and things would be OK again, Jack, really, things would be all right. "I'm not leaving you, Jack, Jack; I'm trying to get you back home. If I were leaving you, I'd never call you like this, from this phone that probably has some of your teen-aged spit still on it."

Then Jack laughed a little and said he had to go to that interview in Sturgeon Bay; he couldn't pass it up. But when I hung up the phone I knew he would come home. I just didn't know when.

It was getting light. In the dark kitchen the windows hung like grey pictures on the walls. I went to look at Carl again. He was still asleep on his side, one cat curled in the curve of his chest, the other behind his knees. I left the house quietly and drove slow into town with the car window open.

Later that morning I was sitting on a green bench with my dad under the big trees in front of the Half Moon Hotel. My father was the same as he had always been, only over the years he had gotten tinier and more pink and white, his hair finer, his memory sometimes fuzzy. He had just taken me to his new favorite place in town for breakfast – there were only four or five choices – and then we had been just sitting there on the bench for a while enjoying the summer sun. There were no buses in Half Moon, but we must have looked like people waiting for a bus and enjoying the wait. We must have looked like May.

"Listen to this, Janet, I heard a guy say this the other day. He was talking about when he was in the Korean War, I think. Anyway, he was talking about some foreign place a long way from here. He said, 'Their flying ants are as big as what we have here for wasps.' Get it, Janet? 'What we have here for wasps'? As if there was some empty space in creation the size and shape of wasps and we Americans were the ones with the good sense to fill that hole with wasps!"

It *was* funny and Dad laughed and slapped my knee to get me to laugh more.

But in a way, I knew how that man was thinking. Only here in this Illinois were there spaces in creation for Carl and Jack and I, spaces the size and shape of each of us grown and old and good.

"Is it Saturday?" Pop asked.

"No, Dad, it's Monday."

"Oh, too bad."

"Why, what is it about Saturday?"

"Well, the Catholics, they do this procession thing when they have their weddings." Pop clapped me on the knee again. "But you know that! You were in one. Oh my god, and it was a good one too! Do you remember what happened?"

"Of course I remember. How could I forget a thing like that. A girl doesn't forget that her skirt came off in her wedding procession." We both laughed and then Dad told the story again, as if I hadn't been there, as if it hadn't happened to me.

We sat there looking at the place where the Catholics could turn onto this street if it were Saturday and if any of them were getting married today. At the end of the street were the fields of corn.

After a while Pop asked me, "What are we doing, setting here, Janet?"

I could answer him. "Waiting for Jack."

About the Author

Martha Bergland's short story, "An Embarrassment of Ordinary Riches," was included in *The Pushcart Prize XII* and listed as one of "One Hundred Other Distinguished Short Stories" in *The Best American Short Stories 1987*. The winner of several Project Grants from the Wisconsin State Arts Board, Ms. Bergland teaches at the Milwaukee Area Technical College.